The eagles and d[...]
The noise had m[...]
of the microcurre[...]
brain. But once they were out of the influence of
the supersonic frequencies they would return.

'How can they see us, Doc?' Pauncho said. 'I
mean, how can the operators of the control boxes
see much through the eyes of the animals in this
dark?'

'I doubt they're using the boxes tonight. It's too
hard to keep the narrow beams locked in under
these conditions. They are probably just
transmitting the code that turns on the juice to
the aggression areas of the brain and letting the
animals attack whatever they come across.'

'I hope so, Doc,' Pauncho said. 'If they can spot
us through the eyes of the birds, we're going to
have a hard time!'

Also by Philip José Farmer in Sphere Books:

MAKER OF UNIVERSES
THE GATES OF CREATION
A PRIVATE COSMOS
BEHIND THE WALLS OF TERRA
THE LAVALITE WORLD
FLESH
LORD OF THE TREES

Keepers of the Secrets

PHILIP JOSÉ FARMER

SPHERE BOOKS LIMITED
30-32 Gray's Inn Road, London WC1X 8JL

First published in Great Britain by
Sphere Books Ltd 1983
Copyright © 1970 by Philip José Farmer

TRADE
MARK

Set in 10/11 Mallard Compugraphic.

Printed and bound in Great Britain by
Collins, Glasgow.

AUTHOR'S NOTE

Although the editors insist upon publishing this work as a novel under my by-line, it is really the work of James Caliban, MD. Doc Caliban wrote this story in the third person singular, though it is autobiographical. He feels that this approach enables him to be more objective. My opinion is that the use of the first person singular would make him feel very uncomfortable. Doc Caliban does not like to get personal; at least, he doesn't like to do so with most people. Even the largest mountain throws a shadow.

Three figures moved in and out of the shadows of clouds and trees. The moon was riding high over the alpine mountain of Gramz in the Black Forest of southern Germany, only a few miles from the Swiss border. Long black clouds raced under it like lean wolves lashed by moonlight beams. Their shadow selves loped over the precipitous western side of Gramz Berg, bounding over the squat and massive stone pile of the castle on top of the mountain, writhing down the jagged slope toward the narrow sheen of the Toll River two thousand feet below.

The three figures were men toiling up the rock-strewn, pine-dotted slant. One was six feet seven inches high. He had the body of a Hercules. His bare head glinted dark-bronzish in the moonlight. If there had been more light, his eyes would have been a very light gray-green with many flecks of bright yellow.

The second man was about six feet tall but seemed much shorter because of the enormous breadth of shoulders and trunk. His arms were disproportionately long and his legs almost freakishly short. The forehead was low and backward slanting. The ridges of bone above his eyes were massive. His nose was a flat wide-nostriled blob, and his chin receded. His ears stuck out like the wings of an owl. His hair was the color of a rusty nail.

The last in line was also six feet tall, but he had the body of a greyhound. His face was that of a handsome

1

fox. His hair was as black and as straight as an Apache's.

The lead man climbed swiftly, though he was burdened with an enormous backpack. The second man, huffing and puffing, called out. He sounded like the grunting of a bear at the end of a long hollow log.

'Have a heart, Doc! You're killing me!'

The third man said, 'Yeah, Doc, maybe you ought to put him on your back, too! Carry old softy Pauncho van Veelar like the baby he is! Forget your pacifier, Pauncho? I brought one along just in case!'

The gorilla-bodied man turned and said, 'Barney Banks! You gotta lotta guts! If it wasn't for you hanging onto my coattails, if I didn't have to drag you along, too, I wouldn't be near so tired! Besides, you ain't got the weight I got to carry, you scarecrow!'

'We'll rest,' the big man said. His voice was deep and resonant, as if his throat contained many small bronze gongs. He sat down on a boulder and waited patiently. Though he could have kept on going without rest at twice the speed all the way to the top, he did not mind stopping. Nor did he mind the bickering of Pauncho van Veelar and Barney Banks. It reminded him of the old days, when their fathers, who looked and sounded so much like them, had carried on a similar running verbal battle.

While the two murmured blistering insults, he looked up the silver-and-black-brindled mountainside. A cloud whipped past the moon, and its lights shone again on the black many-turreted *schloss* still six hundred feet above. The lower wall looked as smooth as the palm of his hand from this distance. But, having gone near it in a helicopter in the daytime, he knew that there were projections and fissures on it. He had studied the photographs and planned the exact course he would take and alternate routes if circumstances barred him from the first.

Doc Caliban reached into a pocket of the vest under his thick jacket and pulled out two pills. He gave one to Barney Albany Banks and one to William Grier van Veelar. They popped them into their mouths and, a few seconds later, felt invigorated.

Doc Caliban began climbing again. The moon raced the clouds and lost but still gained distance across the starry arc. The last six hundred feet were the toughest. Here the mountain became solid perpendicular rock. The three put big flexible plastic discs on their hands and applied these to the rock. The degree of suction was controlled by the degree of pressure on the handles inside the discs.

They reached the junction of rock and the base of the castle. Here they clung to their discs. Their progress was slower from this point on. The alternation of exposed moon and concealing clouds flickered light over them. They seemed like lumps of stone, so minute was their ascent. But as time went by they gained their goal: a narrow opening about sixty feet from the base.

A minute before Doc Caliban pulled himself level with the bottom of the embrasure, a light shone in it.

Doc hung by one disc while he squeezed the other down into a small cylindrical form and stuck it in a pocket in his vest. He then took out a small handweapon from a pocket in his jacket. This was of .15 caliber and shot explosive bullets with a velocity of 4,000 feet a second. The accuracy was, of course, limited, but by holding on the trigger, the entire clip of fifty bullets would be emptied within six seconds. The butt contained a compressed liquid which became a gas ignited by a spurt of another gas into the firing chamber.

Doc Caliban held the gas repeater ready if someone should look out the window. But no sound was heard or object seen from the embrasure. The light, however, remained.

After a few seconds, Doc replaced the gun and took out the disc for his right hand and began his turtlelike climbing. When his chin was above the ledge of the opening, he stopped. The light showed him a narrow landing of stone within stone walls. Opposite was a narrow door of black wood with a tracery of red-painted iron. The embrasure had one vertical bar set in it and a window of glass which would have to be swung inward to be opened.

Hanging by his left disc, Doc Caliban withdrew two long wires about a twelfth of an inch in diameter. He tied one end around the lower part of the iron bar. Then he released the pressure of the disc. He pulled himself upward with one hand by the bar, reached up, and with one hand tied the end of the other wire around the upper part of the bar. After this, he lowered himself until he was below the embrasure, put a disc on his right hand so he could hang on the wall, and pressed a small button in a tiny device in a pocket in his vest.

Fire spurted from the wires around the bar. Doc went back up the embrasure, pulled the bar out and then laid it on the embrasure with its end sticking out. Inside the narrow opening, crouched with his back against one wall and his face almost touching the other, he tested the window with one hand. It did not seem likely that an alarm would be installed on this window, where only eagles could be expected to land. But there was only one way of finding out. He cut the glass with a diamond after applying a suction disc to it. When he had lowered it to the inner wall of the landing, he climbed through. A few minutes later, Pauncho's broad shoulders and big hard stomach came through. He groaned as his shoulders caught on the edges, and Barney, below him, said, 'What's the matter, fatty?'

Barney could not see Pauncho, of course, but he guessed what was happening.

As Barney's head came above the ledge of the embrasure he found himself looking into the savagely grinning chimpanzee face of Pauncho.

'Who's a fatty, Bones?' he said.

'Quit clowning around!' Barney said. 'I'm tired of hanging around here like a bat! I know you like it, since you're half-batty. But I don't! Let me in!'

Pauncho put a huge hand, the back of which was covered with thick dark-red hairs, against Barney's face. 'One shove, and you can solo without wings.'

Doc Caliban said, 'We haven't time for that.' Pauncho backed away, and Barney climbed in. Doc Caliban pulled up the latch of the door, but the door would not swing out. He then started down the steps, the little gas-operated gun in his big hand. Behind him on the stairway, which was too narrow for two men abreast, were Pauncho and Barney. Each held a gun like Doc's.

They went down three complete windings of the corkscrew staircase before coming onto a broader landing. Doc tried the wooden door here, and it opened noiselessly, its hinges having been recently oiled. The room beyond was huge, reached by a short flight of steps leading downward. At one end was a big canopied bed. The walls were naked granite blocks except where covered by huge tapestries. There were a few pieces of massive oak furniture. Heads glared down from the walls: elks, elephants, rhinoceros, African buffalo and American bison, wolf, lion, tiger, leopard, jaguar, kodiak bear. They were fine specimens but nothing extraordinary. They could be found in the game room of any man with money and time and the need to slaughter.

But on a table in a corner, near the huge fire-place on the western wall, was a mounted animal that he had never seen outside some drawings based on speculation and a photograph that could be faked.

'*Tatzelwurm*,' he said.

5

It was a lizardlike reptile with a long slim snakelike body about five and a half feet long. The skin was brownish on top and somewhat lighter on the bottom. Its four legs were very short. The heavy and blunt-snouted head merged into the thick body with no bridge of a neck. The eyes were large and round and a light green.

'What's a *Tatzelwurm*?' Pauncho said. He stood beside the specimen, and the two, except for Pauncho's clothes, would have made a prehistoric tableau. He could have been a Neanderthal and the lizard a left-over from even earlier days.

'It's a reptile that's been reported as living in the Alps,' Doc said. 'There have been too many witnesses with similar descriptions over too long a period of time for any doubt, about its existence. It could be a form of giant salamander or skink. But the longest ever seen was about three feet long. This is a monster. I wonder where Iwaldi got this? And I wonder how many years ago?'

There was enough dust on the furniture and speci-mens to indicate that this room was not much used. Nor was there anything of value for the business at hand.

Caliban, however, went over the room as swiftly as he could, looking for hidden entrances to tunnels and electronic detection devices. A few minutes later, he led Pauncho and Barney out of the room and down the winding staircase. On the next landing, they found a hallway running to the north and walked down it. There were three doors along the hall and one at the end. Caliban looked into the first three and found them empty rooms with piles of boxes and furniture. The door at the end revealed another huge bedroom. This was furnished with expensive tapestries and a bed and table like the one above, but it lacked the mounted heads. The fireplace was glowing with coals, and the bed was in disorder and still bore the impression of a body.

A closet door was behind a tall wooden screen on which was painted a medieval battle scene. The clothes hanging in the closet were those of a woman, but the variety was amazing.

'She sure must go to a lot of costume balls,' Pauncho said. 'Or else she's a collector of historical clothes.'

The closet was big enough to have made a satisfactory bedroom in most houses. By walking down the various racks, the three walked through history, starting approximately at the middle of the seventeenth century. Most of the clothing was preserved in airtight plastic bags filled with gas, probably helium.

This was interesting and somewhat puzzling, but they were not inside the castle for a Cook's tour. Caliban said, 'Go!', being one who hates to waste words, and they left the closet and started toward the door to the hallway.

There was a slight chuffling sound behind them. It was heard only by Doc Caliban, whose ears had been sensitized by a chemical he had invented. He whirled, and the others began to turn as soon as he started to move. A section of the stone wall had slid smoothly aside and out of the blackness leaped huge gray forms. They were Canadian timber wolves, and they uttered no sound except for the click of nails on the stone floor. On top of each of their heads was a hemisphere of some gray material about the size of a ping-pong ball cut in half.

Ten bounded out of the hole, their jaws open and slavering, the white teeth ready to clamp down, driven by jaws powerful enough to take off a man's arm with one bite.

The first wolf, arcing toward Barney, who had been at the end of the line, suddenly found the giant with the dark red hair and the peculiar gray-green-and-yellow eyes at the end of its leap. A hand with muscles like pythons seized the wolf by the throat and Caliban whirled. The wolf shot out of the suddenly opened hand and went past Barney and Pauncho, its tail flicking Barney's face. It crashed into the door and fell in a limp heap.

Caliban kept on whirling, and the edge of his palm struck the second wolf in its midleap and broke its neck with a sound as of an axe chopping a tree.

Pauncho knew the necessity of silence, but he found it almost impossible to throttle himself when he was in a fight to the death. His first cry was like a bull fiddle being strummed way down in a mountain hollow, and the strummings came faster and faster but somewhat higher as the struggle continued. His enormous fists smashed into the tender noses of the beasts or on top of their heads, crushing the delicate hemispheres and stunning the brains beneath. Twice he shot animals with the gun in his left hand. Twice he went down, bowled backward by a body the jaws of which closed on his jacketed plastic chain-mailed arm.

Barney had shifted his gun to his left hand too, and a six-inch knife had suddenly appeared in his right. Like a ballet dancer, he whirled among the wolves, bending, bounding, thrusting. Then he went down with the impact of a huge male on his shoulders, and two others jumped in to savage him.

Pauncho, roaring, kicked one of the wolves so hard in the rear that he raised it off the floor and sent it rolling over the tangle of Barney and wolves. The wolf did not get up again. Then Pauncho seized a tail and dragged the wolf, its legs pumping frantically to keep its grip on the floor, away from Barney. The wolf turned to bite Pauncho, but Pauncho fell on it with his hands around its throat. Another wolf leaped on his back only to be lifted up and smashed against the wall by Doc Caliban.

Barney yelled when the teeth of a wolf exerted very painful pressure on his calf. They would have cut through his muscles if it had not been for the plastic chain-mailed longjohns he was wearing. Barney shot the wolf, rolled away, put up his arm to ward off another wolf, and blew its eye and a good part of its brains out.

Caliban had grabbed two wolves by the throats as they leaped together at him and banged their heads together again and again. A third fastened its teeth around his leg, tearing the cloth of his pants. The pressure of the jaws hurt Doc's leg, but he made no sound. His face expressionless, he dropped the two unconscious wolves and seized the third beast by the ears. He jerked upward so violently he tore the animal's ears off, and it let loose of him and fled back to the hole. But before it reached it, it stopped, stood trembling for a moment, then wheeled and charged Doc again.

Caliban was amazed at its behaviour. Its actions could only be accounted for by some influence from the hemisphere on top of its head.

He charged the wolf and as it rose upward toward his throat he bent over beneath it and then came up with his fist into the beast's belly. It kept on going, but its hind quarters flew up with the impact of the blow and it turned over and landed on its back. It did not get up.

Suddenly, the fight was over. There was silence except for the heavy breathing of Pauncho and Barney. Not once had the wolves uttered even a growl.

Doc Caliban smelled the sting of explosives and the rich undercurrent of blood. There had been a time when he had savored those odors, even though he had not liked killing. Only once in his life, when he had gone mad from the side effects of the immortality elixir, had he enjoyed killing. Now he could not tolerate the odors associated with death once the immediate need for being in their neighborhood was over. He said, 'Let's go!' and they picked up their guns. The section of wall had slid back into place. It was obvious that whoever was controlling it was not going to open it again unless to release another form of death. It was possible that the opening was done automatically, and that they could find the controls to reopen it. But he wanted to get away from here in case the action was not automatic. Besides, alarms would be ringing somewhere in the castle.

Doc wrenched off several hemispheres from the dead animals' heads, and they went down the cork-screw staircase again and came to another landing. For the first time they heard the muffled sounds of helicopters and of rapid fire rifles. Then there was a rumble – a bomb going off? – and, very faintly, screams.

Pauncho laughed one of his surprisingly shrill laughs – he had two different laughs – and said, 'Iwaldi's giving two parties, and he didn't want either one, heh, Doc?'

Doc said, 'It does sound as if he's being attacked on the front. We'll take advantage of whatever happens.'

They walked swiftly down the spiral, their handguns ready. They went down four levels and still had not seen any other life. But the battle noises were louder and they were coming from the front of the castle. Through an open window they heard the *chuff-chuff* of a number of copters. There were several more booms. Grenades, probably.

The backside of the castle was on the edge of the 2,600 foot and almost perpendicular mountainside. The front of the castle was on a much less steep slope. A road ran from the drawbridge down the mountain, snaking back and forth between and through heavy woods. It eventually led to the village of Gramzdorf, where six hundred citizens supported themselves by working for several ski resorts in the winter and farming in the summertime. The ski runs were on the Heuschrecke mountain across the valley from the Gramz.

Wherever the choppers had come from, they had not come from Gramzdorf. Nor could Doc imagine who was attacking Iwaldi.

They went down another level and came out into a huge luxuriously furnished hall. It would have done credit to the magnificent palace of the mad King Ludwig of Bavaria. Iwaldi had been collecting artifacts for many hundreds of years, perhaps thousands of years, though this castle was not built until 1241, if the records were to be believed. But Doc had reason to think that there had been an older structure on which the *schloss* had been erected, and this may have gone back to Roman days. And he also believed that beneath that ancient building, inside the granite of the mountain itself, were extensive halls and shafts, many levels, most of them hacked out of the stone in an unimaginably distant age.

The staircase continued to wind on down, but Doc decided to go toward the source of the noise. He removed from the pack on his back six objects which looked like tennis balls with pins stuck in each. Two he put in his pocket and he gave two each to the others. They went on briskly through hall after hall and room after room, all with furnishings and *objets d'art* that would have astonished scholars in many fields.

Then he stepped behind a massive marble pillar covered with golden filigree. The deafening reports of rapid-fire rifles and pistols were coming from the next room. A man ran into the room and fell on his face. Blood spread out from beneath him.

Another man ran into the room, holding an FN automatic rifle. He stopped, looked around, and gestured to someone out of sight in the other room.

11

Doc whispered, 'They're retreating, clearing the way for Iwaldi.'

Doc could not believe that he would have Iwaldi in his sight so quickly. It had only been four days since an agent had reported seeing Iwaldi in Paris. It had been only three days since Doc had received a report that Iwaldi had flown, via chopper from Freiburg, to the castle of Gramz. Of course, organizing the search for Iwaldi and conducting it had taken five months of hard work. But the lair of Iwaldi had finally been located, and here the millennia-old man had been cornered. But Iwaldi had not survived this long by being careless or minus a sixth sense. It seemed to Caliban that things just could not be quite right if he got that ancient dwarf so quickly.

Part of this feeling came from the awe he could not help feeling for one of the Nine. It was they who had given him the elixir which enabled him, at the age of sixty-six, to be, physiologically, only twenty-five. It was they who had controlled the world for unknown thousands of years. If they did not actually rule it – and they might, for all he knew – they exercised a power that exceeded that of all the combined nations of the world. Doc Caliban, who had turned against them in disgust, could not tell the world the truth. He would not live for more than a day if he came out in the open to proclaim the truth. And, moreover, the world would not believe him. They would think he was insane.

Old Anana, thirty thousand years old at least, was the woman who headed the Nine, and it was she whom he would have liked to have had within the sights of his gun. With her dead, the others would not be quite as awesome and dreadful. But they were dreadful enough, and Iwaldi had killed thousands who had thought to kill him.

Three more men with rifles came in. Doc took one of the tennis-ball like objects from his pocket, waited while he peeked around the massive column, then saw the white hair and long whiskers of the squat dwarf. He got a flash of a face as wrinkled as the neck of a vulture turkey, and the long arms and short thick bowed legs. The dwarf was dressed in a peculiar suit that seemed to be made of badgerskin. Perhaps he wore this for some ritual reason. Or perhaps he was, being so old, hard put to keep warm.

Doc stepped halfway around the column, twisted and then pulled out the three-tenths-of-an-inch pin that extended from the north pole of the little globe, and tossed it. The riflemen began firing almost immediately, but he had whipped back behind the column. Bullets screamed off the marble; chips flew. The three men clung to the side of the column. Then there was a roar half-deafening them as the two gases in the plastic ball mixed. Doc leaped out at once, his gun ready. There was very little smoke from this type of grenade. The riflemen were all lying on their backs or sides, spread out in a sort of petal arrangement.

Iwaldi was nowhere in sight.

Doc at once pulled the pin from his other grenade and tossed it exactly through the middle of the wide and tall arch. It bounced on through, being as resilient as a tennis ball, and six seconds later, it exploded. But Iwaldi and his men were not in sight nor was there any sound of firing from them. Nor was the other party firing.

Doc ran to the archway and looked around its side. The room was a huge one, about one hundred feet by sixty. At the other end, the main entrance, a few heads were beginning to stick out from the side. A number of bodies lay here and there and chairs and massive tables with marble tops had been turned over to provide protection. But Iwaldi and his men were gone.

The men by the main entrance began to fire at him. He slipped back through the archway and gestured to

Pauncho and Barney to follow him. Waiting for a pause in the firing, he leaped across so swiftly he must have seemed a blur to the invaders. They fired again but too late. And the other two, bending over, ran past the space where they would be exposed to the firing when there was another pause.

Someone shouted then. Many boots slapped on the marble floor. Pauncho spun and pulled a pin and bounced a grenade off the side of the archway and into the next room. Before the first had exploded, he had sent a second after it. All three were racing toward the exit at the far end of the room when the blasts came, one, two.

And then three, four.

The last two went off near or under an enormous table of mahogany and marble, twenty yards behind them. It broke in two and soared out of the smoke. The concussion pushed them on through the doorway out of the room and knocked them down.

They scrambled to their feet. Pauncho roared, 'Our grenades and theirs passed each other!'

Doc gestured at Barney, who slipped out his two grenades and threw them, one after the other, at the far archway. One hit the edge and bounced back into the room. The other caromed off at the proper angle. The three stepped around the corner to be out of the direct influence of the explosion.

Two roars succeeded their two as someone tossed in grenades from the other side.

Doc signaled that they should keep on going. They passed through several large rooms and then Doc stopped. He had detected a slight crinkling of a large tapestry hanging on the wall to the right. Lifting the tapestry up, he looked behind it. The wall was of solid stone blocks bound in mortar. Or they seemed to be. But he had seen the stone-block wall in the bedroom upstairs slide away, and the tapestry might have been caught slightly, or bent, when a section behind it closed.

He quickly examined the area behind the tapestry and pressed here and there but nothing happened. Either the opening device was too well hidden, or certain spots had to be pressed in a certain sequence. Or possibly the activator for the opening mechanism was on the other side, and this opening was to be used as an exit only.

He went out from under the tapestry and started away when Barney's sharp metallic voice said, 'Doc!'

Doc wheeled and saw that the tapestry was sagging in the middle. Understanding at once what was happening, he jerked his thumb at a group of large chairs against the opposite wall, and they quickly hid behind one of them. Doc passed out two more grenades to each of them but cautioned them in a whisper to use them only if they could not use their guns. Then he extended a slender flexible telescoping device under the chair and looked through it. But turning it on his end he could rotate the other end within 180 degrees and sweep the room. The end was uptilted, thus giving him a worm's eye view.

A red-headed man stuck his head out first. He was followed by six men, and then, through the doorway through which Doc and his friends had passed, twenty others came. Doc knew then how Iwaldi had disappeared so swiftly. He had taken a secret entrance in the wall of the outer room and gone through the tunnel to this room. The invaders had seen him and followed. Doc was glad that Iwaldi had not then cut back and taken Doc's party by surprise on the flank. But Iwaldi had not wanted to delay for anything. He had wanted to get away as fast as possible.

The invaders carried FN rifles and .45 automatic pistols, and four had hand grenades attached by the pins to their belts. There was even a bazooka team, one man with the tube and one carrying three rockets in a case on his back.

Doc made signs to Barney and Pauncho. They should let the invaders go on by. It was true that three grenades, thrown at once, could catch the whole party together and so dispose of them. But, though he had been compelled to fight them for the sake of survival, he did not know that they were basically hostile to him. Moreover, it would be best to use them to hound Iwaldi.

The party passed through the archway but left one man behind as a rearguard. Doc took out from a little box in his pack a ping-pong-sized, transparent ball and threw it when the man was looking the other way. The man spun on hearing the material break on the stone, looked around, then collapsed. Doc and his men had not even bothered to hold their breaths, since they were outside the influence of the vaporized curare. Doc sped to the man and applied the end of an air-operated syringe to his neck. He struck a sharp blow on the man's chest, and the man began to breathe again. But he was now unconscious and would remain so for half an hour.

Doc told Barney to return to the outer room and find where the secret entrance was. Pauncho appropriated all the man's weapons. Doc searched him for documents or other identification and found nothing. He was not even carrying a wallet.

The tapestry bulged, and Barney called out, 'I've found it!'

'Who couldn't?' Pauncho said. 'They left the door open, right?'

'I could tell you where to put the door, but I'm a gentleman,' Barney said, coming out from behind the tapestry. 'I'll define the term *gentleman* for you when we're not so busy.'

'Would you mind spelling it for me?' Pauncho said. He grinned at Barney. He looked like a chimpanzee who'd just seen a fresh banana. 'Hey, Doc, this Yale graduate's a real sooper-dooper speller. Did you know we were in Korea six months before he found out you don't spell it C-H-O-R-E-A? Haw, haw! Of course, he wasn't too far wrong. Korea was a disease, as far as us marines were concerned.'

'That's a disgusting lie!' Barney said. 'As far as that goes, you thought Korea was in the South Pacific, and you're a Berkeley graduate!'

Doc said, 'Stick something in that door under the tapestry. Not something big enough to make it stick out noticeably. We might want to use it for a getaway.'

Barney looked disgusted, but he was angry at himself for not having thought of the idea. And he did not like Pauncho's grin. He knew his squat buddy was telling him, silently, that he was a dummy.

Doc was thinking how much the two resembled their fathers. Yet neither had gone to his father's college or taken up their professions. Perhaps this was because they resented or even hated their fathers at the same time that they loved them. Both Porky Rivers and Jocko Simmons had been divorced by their wives because they spent too much time away from home on their adventures with Doc Caliban. Both women had remarried, and their husbands had adopted their stepsons. But the real fathers still had visiting privileges, and they came about four or five times a year to take the boys on trips. Doc had met them and even entertained them in his apartment high up in the Empire State Building or on his Lake George estate. The boys had grown up imitating their real fathers because they were mysterious adventurers who roamed the world and did all sorts of fabulous and dangerous deeds. They were the sons of men who had married late in life, and so they had fantasized that they would replace their fathers when these grew too old for the man-killing exploits demanded of them by close relationship with Caliban. The old men had finally retired. But then they had come out of retirement for one last great adventure in Africa, when Doc Caliban was on the trail of the man he believed had killed his beloved cousin, Viscount Grandrith, a man whom most of the world believed to be a purely fictional character and whom the world knew largely by a name that had originated in a non-human language.

Grandrith had not killed Trish Wilde. He had not even known of her existence when she was reported murdered by him. But Grandrith was mad at that time, insane in a peculiar way from the side effects of the elixir of immortality given to him by the Nine in return for certain services. Caliban was also insane because of the elixir's side effects. But he and Lord Grandrith discovered that they were half-brothers; and then Porky Rivers and Jocko Simmons died in their last battle at Castle Grandrith.

Pauncho van Veelar and Barney Banks had had a big shock when they saw Doc Caliban in 1968 after five years' absence. Of course, they had always remarked on how young their 'Uncle Doc' looked. But seeing him again had brought up some very disturbing questions. How could a man born in 1901 still look thirty years old or younger? He should show some signs of aging! And so Doc Caliban, who desperately missed his old sidekicks, no matter how self-sufficient he seemed to others, took their sons into his confidence. They would have joined him just to be able to get into the most exciting life on Earth and to follow in the footsteps of their beloved-hated fathers. But the chance of becoming immortal would have been more than enough inducement.

Barney had picked up two rifles and extra magazines of 20 rounds each. Doc said, 'Thanks,' and inspected his rifle for working order. Pauncho finished taping the mouth, wrists, and ankles of the sleeping guard. Doc said, 'If my suspicions are correct, Iwaldi will be making for his underground labyrinth. He'll probably leave the way open so his enemies will follow him down. They'll find out why he's so hospitable.'

They had just entered the next room when they heard and felt the explosion. The floor quivered, and air moved against their faces. Two rooms on, they came to an entrance made by a section of wall sliding back. Faint streamers of smoke and an odor of dynamite were being breathed from the dark mouth. Doc removed from his vest pocket a cap with a small tube atop it and put it on his head. Then he unfolded dark goggles from the same pocket and put them on. The others also put on caps and goggles, and then they went into the tunnel. This was unlit, but it did not impede them. The device atop the can projected a 'dark light' and their special goggles enabled them to see whatever the light hit. They had contact lenses which would do the same work, but these required time and effort to get in and out, and they preferred the goggles in this situation because they could be ripped off if the situation demanded.

The tunnel curved away from the entrance and then straightened out. The smoke got thicker. They inserted nose plugs to filter it. Thirty feet past the bend, they came to the entrance of a vertical shaft. Doc went down the steel ladder first, his backpack rubbing against the stone wall of the shaft behind him. He counted forty rungs about a foot apart before he stepped onto the bottom of the shaft. A horizontal shaft joined it, leading in an easterly direction. It was designed for dwarfs or designed to make men of normal stature uncomfortable. All three had to duckwalk for thirty yards before they came to a place where they could straighten up. This was a forty-foot square room, carved out of granite, furnished only with corpses.

These were near the opposite doorway. Apparently they had touched off some kind of trap loaded with explosives. Doc counted the bodies. Eight. That left eighteen. The bazooka team was not among them. He would have to be cautious about going too fast, since the survivors would be proceeding slowly now. However, the explosives in that confined area must have deafened and injured others, and the effective number of fighters in their party should be cut down. Also, it was possible that they would get cold feet, for which he could not blame them, and would return. To run head-on into them in these cramped tunnels could be fatal to his small party. But there was nothing to do but push on.

They walked bent-kneed through a thirty-five foot tunnel which ended when it joined another tunnel at right angles to it. Doc squirted some vapor for several yards down both directions. Suddenly, glowing footprints – glowing only because the goggles revealed them – sprang out. But the prints were in both directions, and Doc did not have any way of separating the Iwaldi party's prints from those of the invaders. It was true that Iwaldi was not over four feet five inches high, but his feet were disproportionately large. Nor was there any way of determining the weight of the person who had left prints. The vapor settled on the floor and was illuminated only where there was a difference in elevation of the material of the floor itself. Even a difference of two microns briefly illuminated the powder. There was enough dust on the floor for the boots to make some impressions.

The prints indicated that their makers had been going and coming on both sides of the tunnel at right angles to the one from which they had just emerged.

Doc cast up and down the tunnel for thirty yards. There were many more prints to the right, and then he found a stain of blood on the side of the wall to the right. He turned and beckoned to the two men, who could see him plainly in the radiation cast by their projectors.

'It's possible that they split up and some went the other way,' he said.

Twenty yards further, the tunnel made a turn to the left. After another twenty yards, they found the tunnel almost completely blocked. A section of solid stone, three feet high and twenty long, had thrust itself out of the wall on the right and crushed a number of men against the left wall. Doc removed his pack and shoved it ahead of him while he crawled between the top of the block and the ceiling of the tunnel. He counted eight heads, most of which were above the stone, the bodies being squeezed into forms three inches wide. That left ten ahead, if the party had not split up.

'If I was them, and I'm glad I'm not,' Pauncho said, 'I woulda taken off by now.'

'Maybe you shouldn't try to get through there,' Barney said in a mock solicitous voice. 'With that belly, you'll get stuck, and I won't be able to get by you. You stay here and guard my rear.'

Pauncho chuckled, and the echoes came back from ahead. Doc said, '*Sh!*', but Pauncho whispered, 'Any time I get a chance – '

He stopped when Doc repeated his warning. Then he heard the noises, too.

Pauncho did have some trouble getting his huge belly through, and he was huffing and swearing when he fell off the other end of the block. By then the yelling and screaming of men and the weird shrill cries had increased. They duckwalked swiftly, Pauncho groaning softly and swearing that he would quit drinking beer if he ever got a chance to drink beer again. The tunnel bent at ninety degrees to the right, continued for ten yards, bent ninety degrees to the left, continued for twenty yards, and then they were at the arched entrance to a room so large it could almost be called a cavern.

It was lit only by the flashlights of the men inside but

Doc's blacklight enabled him to see everything clearly. He removed the goggles for a moment so he could get an idea of how the situation looked to the men. The beams shot here and there and then dived for the floor, lay there shining, and were picked up again, though not always by the one who had dropped them. Some of the beams briefly illuminated large birds: white snow owls, golden eagles, bald eagles, African vultures. They swooped through the beams, their eyes flashing redly, their wings beating loudly, their talons outspread. Some closed in on the holders of the flashlights as if they were riding the beam down to their target. The butts of rifles flashed; one struck an eagle on the wing, and the great bird fell out of sight.

No rifles were being fired. Apparently the men were afraid of ricochets. They were using the weapons as clubs. But the birds did not seem discommoded by either the darkness or the lights shining in their eyes. They attacked from all angles, and men went down screaming under their beaks and talons.

Doc replaced his goggles.

The birds uttered no cries whatsoever. They were as silent as the wolves that had attacked Caliban's group in the bedroom. It was this that caused Caliban to look for the tiny hemispheres attached to the tops of the birds' heads.

Doc motioned to his colleagues to retreat with him. They duckwalked back to the end of the block and waited. Barney whispered, 'What's going on, Doc?'

'Keep your rifles ready. We can shoot if we're attacked in here. As to the strange behavior of the animals and birds, I'll explain when I'm certain of its cause.'

The screams went on for about ten minutes and then died out. The only sound was Pauncho's heavy breathing and the ripping of flesh as the birds tore at the corpses. Doc, not wanting to make any noise at all, put his hand on each man's arms and transmitted in Morse with the pressure of his fingers.

'The hemispheres may be electronic devices to control the animals by remote control. It's possible that the operator thinks his enemies are all dead and has shut down control. In which case, we might be able to stroll on by the birds without their attacking us. I say we should try it.'

Barney and Pauncho simultaneously squeezed back, 'You're the boss, Doc. You give the word.'

He transmitted, 'Ordinarily I would. But this is a very bad situation, and I would not blame you one bit if you decided to retreat now so we could fight later – in a situation more advantageous to us.'

'If we go back, will you go back with us?' Barney transmitted.

Doc hesitated and then said, 'No.'

'Then we'll go on with you. Don't you like us, Doc, you want us to miss out on this? We have to earn our immortality.'

Doc smiled slightly, and it was a measure of how deeply he was affected that he allowed his self-control to lapse even this much. Or perhaps it was a measure of his progress in getting rid of the too-rigid self-control of his past. He was trying to act more humanly, or more openly, since being too self-controlled was as human as not being self-controlled enough.

'O.K.,' he squeezed back. 'You cover me from the entrance. If they attack, I'll drop on my back and shoot upward, and you fire over my head.'

He waddled into the room, straightened up, and walked toward the nearest body and the golden eagle feeding on it. The eagle looked fiercely at him and turned on top of the corpse, flapping its wings. Its beak opened as if it were uttering a silent cry. But it did not fly away. Nor did it attack. And the other birds continued to eat after glaring at him and assuring themselves that he was not belligerent.

Doc turned to signal to the two. Barney shouted, 'Look out, Doc!'

He wheeled, bringing up his rifle, having heard the flap of wings at the same time that Barney yelled. The vulture flew at him with beak and claws outspread, and behind him was the thunder of two dozen pairs of wings. All headed toward him.

He fell on his back, firing as he did. The vulture flew bloodily apart and spun to one side under the impact of the bullets. Blood and feathers and flesh spattered Doc. He continued to fire at the great birds, and then the explosions of his colleagues' FN's were added to his. Bullets ricocheted off the walls and the ceiling, wheeing by him, and his face stung from chips of stone. But the birds blew apart from the many high-velocity bullets striking them. And when Doc and the two men had emptied their magazines, they dropped the rifles and began firing with the 15-caliber explosive bullets from their gas guns. Able to see in the blacklight, they had no trouble aiming, and within sixty seconds all twenty-four birds were heaps of feathers.

Doc jumped up and ran toward the entrance of the tunnel as they quit firing and dived into its shelter.

Pauncho said, 'What's up, Doc?' but Caliban did not reply.

He waited for some sign of action, knowing that the renewal of attack by the birds probably meant that the operator had happened to look into the room and see him. Or perhaps it meant that the operator had seen him from the first but had not stimulated the birds until he thought Doc was off his guard. It also meant that the operator could have a form of blacklight, since Doc had stayed out of range of the beams of the flashlight still operating.

Nowhere was there any evidence of TV cameras or

one-way windows, but it would be easy to simulate rock.

There was a groaning behind them and a trembling of the floor. They turned to see the huge stone block withdrawing into the wall. The heads of the collapsing bodies struck the stone with a plop.

Doc nodded, and they got up and walked across the room, pausing only by the bodies to shove an extra magazine into their capacious jacket pockets. The exit was another archway at the far wall. They looked down its round length. Doc wondered why the tunnel was round instead of square, as all the others had been. It went for at least forty yards before making a turn. The roundness might preclude any section of the wall sliding out to crush them. At least, the interior was smooth, seemingly carved out of the granite. But material in paste form, looking like stone, could have been spread over to cover up the lines of demarcation of a separate piece. He whispered to them, and they walked to the tunnel and entered, crouching. They held their rifles across their bellies so that the muzzle and stock extended past their sides.

They had gone ten yards when the wall to their right crumbled and flew outward, propelled by a block of stone. The mass squealed as it slid across the floor – but not loudly, indicating that the bottom was lubricated – and then the three were knocked sidewise. But the block stopped short with a crash; their rifles acted as rigid bars to hold the block back. And it was evident that there would be no more pressure put on them. The rifles had bent just a trifle but showed no signs of increasing buckling.

Doc crawled over his rifle and scooted on out past the block. He felt naked without the rifle to keep off the block, even though he knew that the three already wedged in were doing their work. Pauncho and Barney came after him with Pauncho snorting indignantly because Barney was making cracks about hippos in subways. But when they were out of danger, they sat down and wiped the sweat off.

Barney said, 'Do you think – ?' He stopped. Of course, Doc Caliban had no way of knowing whether or not there would be more such traps ahead. And they now had no rifles. They could go back and pick some more up. But, if they were being observed, the block could be withdrawn as soon as they went past the wedged rifles. And it could then be slammed in again with an excellent chance of catching them.

Barney and Pauncho had both thought of this, because Pauncho said, 'I'll stay there holding on to a rifle and make sure that if the stone's moved, I'll be there to catch it again.'

'Three rifles were strong enough to withstand it,' Doc said. 'I don't know that just one would do it.'

'They're close enough I could reach out and grab two,' Pauncho said. 'And Barney could hold the other.'

Doc looked at the block. This one was so much closer to the ceiling that crawling on its top was ruled out. It was as long as the other, and it had slid out when the three were halfway along its length.

'No,' Doc said. 'It could be withdrawn and slid out before we could reach the rifles. There's nothing to do except go ahead.'

Barney and Pauncho looked dismal. Doc Caliban kept his face expressionless. It hurt him to see them express any kind of faint-heartedness or lack of faith in him. Yet his reaction was illogical whereas theirs was founded on a realistic attitude. They certainly were not cowards or easily downcast. His little experience with them had convinced him of that. Moreover, they had fought together in the worst of the Korean fighting, had escaped together from a Chinese prisoner-of-war camp, and both had won many medals for valor (though none for good conduct). After the war they had returned to school to get their higher degrees. And they had formed a business which had taken them into South America, where they had been captured by bandits and had again escaped. They did not lack courage or resourcefulness.

His own reaction was a hangover from the past, when he had gotten from their fathers a never-diminished gusto and optimism. They had never faltered. Or they had seemed not to falter. Perhaps they were more self-controlled and would have been ashamed to let him see their dismay. Their sons were more open, less vulnerable to shame. Moreover, if he, who prided himself on his logical behavior, was not doubtful about pushing on, then he must be missing something in his own character.

Doc Caliban thought, Well, not really. It's just that I know that I have more capabilities than they do.

Now was no time for soul-searching. He could do that when he retired to that hidden stronghold which had once been in the far north but which he had relocated at the bottom of a lake. Lately, when he had retreated, he had ceased to work on scientific devices and had taken to pursuing Oriental philosophies and their techniques.

He shook his head. Pauncho said, 'What's the matter, Doc?'

Doc put his hands on their wrists and squeezed a message. Then he said, loudly, 'We'll go ahead, take what comes, play it by ear!'

He turned and Pauncho got on one side and Barney on the other as they started across the room, which was about twenty feet high, sixty long, and forty wide.

Doc took two steps, whirled, and flashed back into the tunnel, sped crouching down it, and dived for the nearest rifle between the wall and the stone. Having seized it, he turned over and slid under it, releasing it only when Barney grabbed it. The two had started immediately after him but they were a few seconds behind since he was so swift. To any watcher he must have seemed almost a blur.

Pauncho, who was three times as strong as Barney but not as quick on his feet, caught up with Barney and grabbed his rifle. In a short time, they each had hold of a gun.

They waited for a moment. That the block had not withdrawn and then slammed in when Doc made his dive seemed to indicate that it was not being remote controlled. A watcher should have been startled by Doc's sudden return and operated the controls in sheer reflex.

It was also possible that the renewed hostility of the birds had come from an automatic mechanism. Doc had triggered off an alarm, perhaps by cutting across a beam.

While Pauncho braced himself between two rifles, and Barney gripped one, Doc slid out and then duck-ran back to the room. He returned with three more rifles. The two took them while Doc gripped the two rifles jammed against the wall and then he dived out and away, just in case there was a remote controller. The stone block did not move.

This room was without furniture or decoration except for a black, red-headed eagle, twice as large as a man, painted on a wall, and a ceramic container which might have been used for bathing small humans. The archway led to another round tunnel, but this was large enough for even Doc Caliban to stand erect in. At irregular intervals along the tunnel, about three feet up, were painted the symbols – squares with looped corners – which the Finns called *hannunkaavuna* and the Swedes *St. Hans's arms*. Doc knew this symbol well. It was carved on the staff which the Speaker for the Nine carried during the annual ceremonies in the caves in the mountains in Central Africa. The upper half of the staff bore a carved *ankh*, the cross with a circle on top, a symbol as ancient as Egypt.

The *hannunkaavuna* made him think briefly of Grandrith. That tall man with the black hair, gray eyes, handsome near-aquiline face, and Apollo-like body with its Herculean strength – his half-brother – should be near the coast of Gabon now. He would land there and proceed on foot across Central Africa, sticking largely to the belt of the rain forest, where few humans would see him. And then he would come up onto the bank of the mountains which held the caves of the Nine, and he would do what he could there. If he was confined to scouting and spying, he would wait until his brother could join him in an attack on the Nine during the annual ceremonies. If he had a chance to kill one of the Nine, he would do so.

The memory of pain twinged him in the back of the neck and elsewhere. His fight with Grandrith had not been without loss and agony.

They got out of the tunnel without incident. Pauncho wiped sweat off his shelving brow and said, 'Whoo!'

Barney said, 'I kept expecting the side of the wall to jump out at us.'

Doc looked around. This room had hexagonal corners and was painted with many scenes of long-bearded squat little men fighting crocodile-sized creatures looking exactly like the stuffed *Tatzelwurm*. The focus of the battle was a big pile of gold rocks. A twilight illumination came from naked plastic bulbs set in widely separated brackets on the walls. Wires ran from them to black boxes on the floor.

Pauncho said, 'Listen, Doc, do you think that once there may have been big whatchamaycallems, and these gave rise to the legends of the dragons?'

'Your guess is as good as mine,' Caliban said, and he led them to the next archway. This was painted black, and the tunnel was black. They proceeded ten yards

29

when they came to a hole in the center of the floor. Doc pointed his headlight down it, making sure that his rifle was still held at the proper angle across his belly. The shaft went straight down for about twenty feet and then became a hole in the ceiling of another tunnel. A section of wooden ladder lying flat on the floor was visible.

The atomizer revealed that someone had gone down the shaft by putting their back to one wall and their feet against the other. It also indicated footprints going on in this tunnel, but the light from the prints was not as bright as that on the walls of the shaft.

'It could be another trap,' Doc squeezed on Barney's arm. Barney transmitted the same message to Pauncho.

'We're playing follow-the-leader,' Barney squeezed back. His thin foxily handsome face looked eager. Pauncho was grinning like an orangutan dreaming of durian fruit.

Iwaldi seemed to be going to the lower levels. At least, that would be the natural direction for him to go when his home was invaded. Perhaps he did not know that his traps had killed all of one party of invaders and that just three men were tracking him. Perhaps he did, and he was crouching in some room and watching them even now, waiting for the proper moment so he could press a button or pull a lever or just watch while an automatic trap was sprung.

Doc leaned over and dropped his rifle, butt first. It struck and toppled over. He waited. Nothing happened. There was nothing to do but go down the shaft then. Near its bottom he removed a suction disc from his pocket, stuck it against the shaft wall, and lowered himself by his left hand down from the shaft, his legs drawn up. He swung like a gibbon from a branch, turning to take in the round tunnel which ran for ten yards in either direction and then curved out of sight. The ceiling was eleven feet from the floor, and the greatest distance between the walls was twelve. There were eight bulbs on brackets along the walls.

'How is it, Doc?' whispered Pauncho.

Caliban looked up. The ugly but congenial face hung over him.

'Only one way to find out,' he said. He released his grip on the handle of the disc, it fell, he grabbed it, and he dropped down to the floor. But his other hand had his gasgun out before his feet struck the stone.

Pauncho came down, grunting, and then Barney.

The moment Barney landed, the world seemed to tilt. Doc made a leap forward for the shaft with his left hand, which still held the disc, extended. And when the disc slapped onto the inner edge of the lip of the shaft, he squeezed down on the handle. The disc held, and he hung there, while the ladder, his rifle, and his two friends went down the slope of the tunnel, which had suddenly dropped and was rapidly becoming vertical.

Sick, he looked down past his feet while Pauncho and Barney, their fingers grabbing for a hold on the smooth stone – or what seemed like stones but could not be – hurtled downward. And then they were gone around the bend, shot out of the gigantic chuteychute. The rifle went with them, and the ladder, bending at a number of places like a wooden snake, shot out by their side.

Panicked though they must have been, neither had screamed or yelled. Pauncho had groaned, and Barney had hissed between clamped teeth, but that was all.

Doc hung there, rotating slowly by the turning of his wrist. He could swing himself up and get his feet against the wall of the shaft and so climb back up to its top. Or he could swing out and back until he had enough momentum and then release the disc and land on the edge of the newly formed vertical shaft and go on down this tunnel. Or he could then climb down the chutey-chute, using the discs and see what was down there. It seemed certain that Iwaldi would be waiting for him there, but he could not abandon his colleagues, not unless he knew for certain that he could help them by action elsewhere.

Within a minute, he was going down the shaft of the trap. When he came to the bend he proceeded more slowly. He lifted the goggles for a moment and, seeing that there was light ahead, left them up. He could see only a whitewashed wall ahead, but when he got to the end of the tube and looked down, he saw Pauncho and Barney.

Below them was another shaft about twenty feet wide and so deep he could not see the bottom. The shaft was in the center of a large room which seemed to be the storehouse for hundreds of wooden brightly painted statues. These ranged from beautiful nudes and fully clothed humans and dwarfish peoples to dragons to elk to wolves to badgers to monsters of various sorts. The light came from a dozen glass bulbs on top of stone lamps.

Pauncho and Barney were at the bottom of a net. This was composed of many thin and apparently sticky cords. Their weight had pulled the net, which originally had been stretched across the top of the shaft, to a bag-like shape with them at the bottom and about twenty feet down the shaft. They were struggling and cursing in low tones, but their efforts only entangled them more thoroughly in the cords. Seeing Doc Caliban, they stopped thrashing around.

'Get me out of here, Doc,' Barney said. 'This guy's so hairy, he's making me itch.'

'Yeah, get me out of here,' Pauncho said. 'He's so bony he's cutting me.'

Doc did not answer. He began to swing back and forth until he had enough momentum. He released the pressure on the disc handle as he started an outward swing, and he landed on the edge of the shaft. Neither of the two made a sound, though it might have been expected that Doc would teeter back and fall into the net with them. His toes only struck the lip of the shaft. But he snapped himself forward and then was solidly on the floor. He turned and began to pull on the net, hauling up the four hundred and seventy pounds of the two men and the hundred pounds of the net as if they were a minnow on a string.

The sticky cords clung to his hands, but he just walked backward, pulling the two over the edge with a bump and a scrape that brought groans from them. After they were on the floor, he managed to pull his hands loose and then he started the tedious and slow task of freeing them.

When they were out of the net, Pauncho and Barney were as dirty looking as coal miners at the end of a shift. The dark brown substance had smeared their clothes, faces, and hands.

'One thing I'll say,' Barney muttered. 'You look just as good dirty as you do clean. Maybe better because it's more natural.'

Pauncho's thick teeth flashed in a grin. 'As an authority on dirt, your opinion is to be valued. It takes one to know one, as they say.'

'Takes one what to know what one?' Barney said.

'If you two will quit your clowning around now,' Doc Caliban said, 'we'll proceed. Though where I don't know.'

From a pocket in his vest he took an object the size and shape of a large pocketwatch. Its face bore a number of dials and graduated markings and also a thin tube with a red column, like a thermometer. The others did not comment. They knew that this was a device with several functions. One of them was to detect objects of a certain shape and density. The device could be set to register when such and such an object was near its field of radiation. Doc now adjusted it by turning a small wheel on its back, and then he advanced down the room holding it out before him.

If there was anything immediately behind the walls or under the floors or above the ceiling, this detector would send a pulse of yellow light up and down the column on its face. The drawback of the detector was that it could not be used in the near vicinity of guns and knives or other considerable masses of metal. It registered the metal even if its radiating field was directed away from the metal. There was a certain amount of back radiation, an echo as it were, and this detected the metal. So Doc Caliban had to give his pistol and knife to Pauncho to carry while he preceded them by thirty feet.

He stopped at a wooden ladder sticking out of a shaft and the two halted with the same distance maintained between them and their leader. He swept the detector around and then went down the ladder. They followed a minute later. The next level down was a long corridor hewn out of solid granite. It ran for as far as they could see in both directions, and it was well lit with naked electric light bulbs on iron brackets about five feet from the floor and spaced about forty feet apart.

Doc sprayed some more of the atomized differential-level substance around. It revealed many footprints, but the freshest seemed to go off to the right, so he elected to go that way. They passed tools lying on the floor or propped against the walls: picks with broken handles or worn points; great sledges, bars with chiseled edges, brooms. Some of them looked as if they had been lying here a long time. Then they came to a broad staircase cut out of the rock. It led down for about sixty feet at a steep angle. They went down it, still guided by the electric light bulbs, and came to a room at least a hundred feet square and forty high.

Doc stopped, and Pauncho and Barney, forgetting

that they were not to get close, almost bumped into him. The red column in the center of the face changed to a bright yellow light which pulsed.

Doc told them to move back, and the light went back to its quiescent state. Barney whistled softly and said, 'Looks like they had a fight sometime ago, doesn't it? A long time ago!'

The footprints were plain here. The dust was so thick that it rose with every step. Pauncho almost strangled trying to keep from sneezing while Barney choked trying to keep from laughing at Pauncho's desperate grimaces.

There were about ten complete skeletons and parts of others scattered around the room. Rusty swords, knives, and double-headed axes lay under the dust, many still clutched by bony hands. Some of the skulls had been cracked or caved in; an axe was still wedged in the top of a skull.

Doc said, 'Most of them were dwarfs. And an early type of *Homo sapiens*. Look at the thickness of those bones, the huge supraorbital ridges.'

The fresh footprints led through one of six archways. Doc went through this cautiously, ready to jump back at the slightest sign of anything suspicious. The room beyond was immense and lit by bulbs in brackets secured to the granite walls. There were more skeletons and axes and swords. And in the center of the room, sitting on an oaken high-backed ornately carved chair on a granite slab, was a figure.

They approached slowly, though it was obviously a corpse.

It was a very old corpse, a mummy. Its white hair fell over its shoulders and its white beard covered its lap and its knees. The dark eyes stared at them.

It wore a cap like a dunce's crown and leather garments and leather boots with curled-up toes. The brown, wrinkled, and heavily veined hand held a golden scepter with six diamonds inset on the polygonal knob of gold at the end of the scepter.

On the slab and around the oaken throne were many figurines of stone about a foot high. They represented a squat, hairy people: males and female adults and some children. They were dressed in clothes similar to that on the mummy. There were a few figurines of animals, mostly badgers, but two were of some sort of monster.

'What do you make of it, Doc?' Pauncho asked.

Pauncho did not expect an answer. But Doc said, 'I am not sure. The mummy looks much like Iwaldi, as you know from my description and my sketch of him. And the figurines are modeled after his people. How this man came to his death, why he's been preserved, I don't know. But you must remember that Iwaldi's people are – were – some sort of dwarfish Caucasoids with a slight Mongolian mixture somewhere along the line. They're the little people who gave rise to the tales of gnomes, kobolds, and even trolls. I'm sure of that. They did a lot of mining and tunneling, and if my theory is correct, they survived in Germany and some parts of Scandinavia up to 1000 A.D. Then they were absorbed or just died out. Iwaldi kept on living. He would, of course, being one of the Nine. And he had this castle built over the ancient stronghold of his race during the medieval period. Though I think he also was the one who built the earlier fortress on which the castle was based.

'This man here may have been some king, perhaps a son of Iwaldi. If we get Iwaldi alive, maybe we can find out about all this. But I would prefer that we kill him. The moment we get the chance to. That old man is too wily, too dangerous, to let live for more than the time it takes to cut his throat.'

He quit talking, and the oppressive silence returned. Pauncho shifted uneasily. The fierce-eyed and long-bearded figure seemed to have moved, though he knew it was an illusion. For the first time, he became aware of the millions of tons of stone over his head. The silence was as heavy as the stone. He was so awed by this that he whispered his feelings to Barney. Barney might have laughed at another time and place, but that he did not do so now showed that he felt much the same as Pauncho.

Doc gestured at them to follow him. He held the detector out ahead of him. Its light was flashing yellow, but the masses of iron weapons were responsible for that. He passed through a tall archway into another room which was filled with digging tools and swords and axes, all neatly stacked in piles along the wall. He chose to go down another broad staircase of stone steps. Footprints led away from it, but footprints also went down it and these seemed to be fresher. The stairs went on and on. Doc counted a hundred, then two hundred, then three hundred with no end in sight. The bottom was hidden somewhere in the shadows below. Along the wall there were bulbs which had been set much further apart.

Moreover, the walls began to move in closer, and the way slowly curved to the right. Then it straightened out for a hundred steps, after which it curved to the left.

'I wonder how far down these diggings go?' Pauncho whispered to Barney. 'If this Iwaldi geezer is 10,000 years old, he may have started digging back then. The whole mountain could be honeycombed.'

Abruptly, the stairs ceased. Doc waved the detector back and forth before the huge oaken door before them. The column in its face was red.

'Hey, Doc!' Pauncho said. 'Those hinges are gold!'

Doc signaled and Barney handed him the knife. Doc touched the golden latch on the door with the knife as if he expected an electrical spark to leap out. Nothing happened. He slipped on the goggles and examined the door and the latch under the 'blacklight.' Then he raised the goggles and said, 'We'll have to take a chance. Stand way back, you two.'

The door swung outward, revealing a cavernous room beyond. This was lit with the ubiquitous bulbs. It seemed to be a storehouse for many things: battle-axes, swords, cuirasses, and leggings, oaken and stone chests, many of them open and glinting with gold bars or gleaming with jewels. There were also statues, ranging from a foot high to life size, carved out of stone or formed from gold and silver. Some were of well-proportioned humans, some of the squat and muscular and thick-calved dwarfs, some of animals, of monsters.

The three walked slowly into the chamber, pausing to look at but not to touch the wealth strewn everywhere. Some of the chests contained coins and paper money of many nations.

Doc kept his attention on the fresh footprints in the dust. These led straight across the immense room toward a set of three arches at the far end. But before they reached them, they halted. On their right, set into the wall, was a steel framework with steel bars. This was at the entrance to a small cell cut out of the stone.

Pauncho and Barney said, simultaneously, 'Wow!'

Doc Caliban's face did not lose its expressionlessness. But a close observer might have noticed those peculiar yellow-flecked eyes narrow.

A young man and a young woman were staring at them from behind the bars.

It was the woman who had caused the two men to express delight, surprise, admiration, and desire.

'Your cousin has finally got some real competition,' Pauncho said to Caliban.

The woman's hair was long and loose and of an unusually deep red. Her skin was very clear and white, and her eyes were large and violet. Her only makeup was a bright red lipstick. She wore heavy hiking clothes

38

and boots, but they were tight enough to reveal a superb figure.

The man was wide-shouldered and muscular but very short. He had black hair and brown eyes and a handsome face.

The woman's voice was throaty and caressing even though she was evidently under heavy stress. She gripped the bars and said, 'My God, where did you come from?' and then, 'Please get us out of here!'

The young man had also grabbed hold of the bars, but he did not say anything.

Doc Caliban looked past them. The cell was furnished with a double bunkbed and some light blankets and pillows, a washbowl with a pitcher of water and a glass, an open toilet bowl, and a stone shelf on which were two trays with dishes on which were the remnants of food.

'Did Iwaldi take the key to this lock with him?' Doc said.

'Who?' the man said.

'The old dwarf,' Doc Caliban replied.

'He went thataway,' the woman said, pointing her finger at the far end. She smiled, but she was evidently trying to be brave. Her fingers were white where she was clutching the bars.

'How many men did he have with him?' Doc said.

'Ten,' the man said. His speech was, like the woman's, Received Standard English – that of an educated Londoner.

Pauncho and Barney were pulling rolls of thin wires from their vest pockets. Doc raised his hand as if to check them, then let it drop. The cell and its prisoners might be an elaborate booby trap of some sort, but the only way to find out was to try to free them. The two wrapped several turns of the wires around the more slender bars which held the lock to the door. They pressed the button on the battery in their pockets;

flame spurted out from around the wires; the bars and the lock were removed with a yank. Pauncho pulled the barred door open and said, '*Exitez-vous, madame.*'

She smiled ravishingly at him; Pauncho, ravished, smiled back.

The man introduced himself as Carlos Cobbs and the woman as Barbara Villiers, his fiancee. They both taught archeology at the university in London. They had been digging on the mountainslope three days ago when they were captured by the dwarf and his men.

Doc thought at first that they meant that Iwaldi's men had picked them up near the castle. But they said they had been digging in the woods near the bottom of the massive stone cap on which the castle rested. The earth had fallen in at the bottom of their trench, and they had gone in with it. Their shovels and picks had broken through the top of a tunnel. Exploring the tunnel, they found that it was part of an immense labyrinth of many levels.

They had pushed on, fascinated because they had come across stone figurines and the skeletons of men who were obviously early paleolithic. And then some men had captured them and brought them here, despite their protests. After a while, a strange long-bearded dwarf had appeared and questioned them. Barbara called him The Mountain King and said these were his halls.

'He wouldn't let us go,' she said. 'He – what'd you say his name was. Iwaldi? – said we were spies and that he'd kill us. But not before he found a use for us, since he didn't believe in wasting anything. He kept muttering something about the nine. Just the nine. Nine what?'

Doc did not reply. He entered the cell and prowled around with his detector in hand. Then he came out and said, 'If I were you two, I wouldn't report this to the local authorities. Or any authorities. I'd just quietly get out of Germany and get back to London. I know you can't forget this, but you should act as if you had.'

'Really?' Carlos Cobbs said. 'Why should we?'

'You would probably die very soon after you started to talk about this. There is another group which is out after Iwaldi's hide – and mine – which would shut you up the hard way. Hard for you, easy for them.'

'And who are you?' Barbara said.

'Your liberator,' Doc said. He was thinking that he should send a radio message to his cousin in London to check on these two as soon as he got back to the village. 'Barbara Villiers?' Barney said, smiling. 'An old and . . . uh . . . well-known name. You aren't related to the late Duchess of Cleveland, Countess Castlemaine, are you?'

The woman smiled back at him and became twice as beautiful. 'You mean the wicked woman who was born in 1641, the daughter of Viscount Grandison? The mistress of Charles II, John Churchill, and William Wycherley, not to mention others common and great?'

'Yes,' Barney said.

She laughed and said, 'Yes, I'm related to her. But I don't have a title. I'm just a commoner.'

'You're true royalty – esthetically speaking,' Pauncho said.

Barney glared at him.

'Don't you wish you'd said that?' Pauncho said, sneering at Barney.

'We're going after Iwaldi,' Doc Caliban said. 'That'll be very dangerous. Besides, I don't want to have to worry about you when the fireworks begin. I suggest that you go back the way we came.'

'Won't that be dangerous, too?' Barbara said. She was looking him up and down and evidently liking what she saw. Doc felt uncomfortable and cursed himself for being weak enough to experience the feeling. He never

41

got over it. He always attracted women, and he always felt uneasy at their admiration. What was worse, he now knew why he got uneasy, and he did not like that at all. After his final encounter with Lord Grandrith in that old castle in the Cumberland, when he had been invalided with a broken neck and was regrowing some rather roughly removed skin and flesh, he had done some deep self-probing.

'Either way is dangerous,' he said. 'But the trail blazed is always less dangerous than the trail to be blazed. Generally, anyway.'

She looked at Carlos Cobbs. 'I'd feel safer if we were with them even if we might run into that dirty old man and his gang.'

Carlos Cobbs shrugged. He said, 'Anything you say, my dear.'

'We can't spare any guns,' Doc said. 'Pick up one of those swords or an axe and stay well behind us.'

'Maybe one of us ought to stay close with the lady and see she doesn't come to any harm,' Pancho said. He grinned at the titian-haired beauty and managed to look even more like a baboon.

'If she stays with you she will come to harm,' Barney said. 'Just looking at you is enough to bring anybody down with a fatal case of the uglies.'

Doc walked away with Barney and Pauncho a few steps behind and the couple following them. He halted before the archway, swept his detector back and forth, and then started through. He felt the floor dip and leaped high into the air like a scalded cat. The detector flew out of his hand as he grabbed for the rough stone along the edge of the point of the archway. Even though his leap took him above the heads of his two men, his fingers could not find a purchase on the stone. He fell back and into the hole below him and after Barney and Pauncho. Their yells were coming up the shaft even as he hurtled through the hole. He saw Cobbs and the woman staring open-mouthed and pale at him, and then the walls of the shaft were the only thing he could see.

Far below came a splash, then another splash. And then it was not so far below, and he plunged into icy water.

He went down deep, but his fall had been perhaps fifty feet, enough to kill a man if he struck the water at the wrong angle. His hard heavy boots took the major part of the energy of the impact. Even so, he was half-stunned. But he had secured the cap with the blacklight device onto his head by holding it with one hand, and he switched that on. Then he slipped his goggles down onto his eyes, sliding it over the skin to keep the water out, and held tightly with the other. As he rose toward the surface, he removed two plugs from a vest pocket and slipped these into his nose. He began breathing through them immediately. They strained oxygen from the water quite efficiently, and he breathed the carbon dioxide out through his mouth.

There was no light down here, and he would have been blind if it had not been for his black-light projector and goggles. Even so, the water seemed to have a suspension of plant growth or perhaps of dirt and he could not see far. But he did make out Pauncho's form and when he had swum near enough for Pauncho to see him, Pauncho gestured outward. Doc swam even closer and could then make out Barney's shadowy figure. In a moment, Barney had swum close.

Both had retained their caps with the projector and their goggles, and they had also inserted into their nostrils the filters. But the icy water was rapidly numbing them.

Doc reached into another pocket and removed an object the size and shape of a boy's marble. He popped it into his mouth, chewed on it, and then swallowed it. A minute later, he began to feel warm. The sense of disorientation that had started to slip through him disappeared. The pill not only provided a source of energy the output of which was proportionate to the demand for warmth, but it fought shock.

He reached the surface but could not stick his head into the air. The water at this point boiled into the ceiling of rock. He and his two colleagues could only stay under and let themselves be taken away by the powerful current. There was no use fighting against it. Even Doc Caliban's massive muscles, anchored to a skeleton almost twice as thick as a normal human being's, could not have made progress against that force.

For approximately five minutes, as registered by the hands of his wristwatch, they were swept between stone walls that came closer and closer. This narrowing of the channel also increased the power of the current. They sped by walls of granite worn smooth by other rocks tumbled along in the past by the river. They kept hold of each other's hand so they would not be separated, and they went around and around as if they were on a dancing streamer around a maypole. But then they began to get cold again, and they had to swallow another energon.

He had one pill left apiece. After the effect of that was gone, their chance for survival was small. Unless – At that moment he heard a roar, and suddenly the water was boiling. A sharp ridge of stone passed a few inches below his drawn-up legs, then he was sliding on an apron of slick rock and then he was half in the air, half in the water, falling and turning over and over. Pauncho's hand was torn from his; a second later, he struck something. His ribs hurt so much that he could not repress a gasp, and water choked him.

When he awoke, he was lying on a muddy bank and was cold, cold, cold.

He sat up and began coughing. A shape appeared out of the darkness. He got to his feet as swiftly as he could but with agonizing slowness. A voice rumbled, 'It's me, Doc. Take it easy.'

He felt his head. His projector was still here. But his goggles were gone. Then his eyes became more adjusted to the dark and he saw that he was on a mud bank that sloped gently for several yards and then rose at ninety degrees for about forty feet. The sky was paler up there. The side of a mountain hung over them on the opposite side; the less precipitous slope was on the other side.

'Where's Barney?' he said.

Pauncho grunted like a sick hog and said, 'He's trying to find a way out of here. You all right, Doc?'

Caliban felt his side. 'I think I cracked some ribs. I won't know until I get back to Gramzdorf.'

'I thought you were a goner. I saw you slam into that boulder at the bottom of the falls.'

Doc could hear the muted roar of the cataract to his left. They must have gone quite a distance downstream before making this bank.

He swallowed another energon. When he started to feel warm again, he said, 'Let's go after Barney.'

They walked into a side street of the little village of Gramzdorf just before dawn. They were no longer cold and wet and dirty and hungry. But they went silently and stealthily and studied the outside of the inn, at which they were guests, for a long time before entering.

Doc had resumed his disguise of Mr. Sigurdsson, the old Norwegian tourist, and Barney was wearing a false red beard and red wig in his guise as a Mr. Benjamin. Pauncho wore contact lenses to change the color of his gray-blue eyes; he had a huge blue-black beard and his hat was jammed down to hide his enormous supra-orbital ridges and his slanting forehead.

At this time of the year, when most of the snows were melted, there were few tourists. The locals, who stayed inside the village to work at the inns and the ski slides and associated businesses in winter, had retreated to their farm-houses. The clerk on duty in the lobby was asleep on his stool. The three walked past him and took the stairs to the third floor, the top floor. Doc inserted the slender tube of his see-around-a-corner and twisted it to inspect the front room from one wall to the next. Then he stuck another tube through the keyhole and pressed a bulb, pulled it out, and reinserted the *saac*, as he called it.

A little box attached to the opposite wall was flashing an orange light. That meant that it had photographed no one entering the room, and that, presumably, it was safe to enter.

Barney, who had been at the end of the hall and looking out of the window, signaled Doc. When Doc got there, he saw two figures coming down a side street: Carlos Cobbs and Barbara Villiers.

Doc Caliban was gone like a rabbit scared by a coyote. Though six feet seven and weighing more than three hundred, he moved as swiftly and as lightly as a tiger. He was down the hall, down the steps, and out onto the lobby just as the couple entered. His timing was precise. The two had no chance to get away if they had wanted to do so. Doc had considered not revealing himself so that he could watch the couple when they thought they were safe. But his own great size and difficulty of disguise for Pauncho van Veelar would also make it easy for the two to recognize them. Besides, he wanted information now, and he did not feel that the waiting game was the one to play at this time.

So he spoke to them in his own voice as they approached.

The jaws of both dropped, and their eyes were wide. But both recovered swiftly. Cobbs did not try to smile, but Barbara managed a brilliant and lovely smile. 'I'm so glad!' she said, advancing with her arms open. 'So glad! And so overwhelmed! I thought you were dead!

You dropped into that awful hole and were gone! But the others? Are they. . . ?'

'All right,' Doc said. 'Would you mind coming to my room? There are some things we have to establish.'

'Why not in the morning?' Cobbs said. 'We're very tired. With good reason, as you know.'

'I would think your curiosity would be too great for you to think of sleep,' Doc Caliban replied. 'You must have seen some things that you would have thought could not exist. And Iwaldi. Didn't – '

'Oh, yes, darling!' Barbara Villiers said, placing a lovely white hand on Cobb's arm. 'He's absolutely right! Besides, why is he disguised as an old man? I'm dying to find out! There must be some tremendous mystery here! I couldn't sleep thinking about that! I don't think I could sleep anyway, not with that mad goblin on the loose yet!'

Doc said, 'The mad goblin. A good description indeed of Iwaldi. Will you go with me?' and he turned as if he fully expected that they could do nothing else.

They followed him up but stopped short when they saw Pauncho and Barney standing before the door. Cobb said, 'Who – ?' and then, 'Very good disguises those! But those long arms and that nose and mouth! No, I think I'd recognize him anywhere no matter what!'

Doc unlocked the door and let the others through and then locked the door and secured a little box against the upper part of the door with a disc. Barney had turned off the mechanism that was flashing a light and was removing the film.

Pauncho said, 'What about a drink to warm us up and give us courage to face the morning sun? I thought I'd never see it again.'

All took some brandy except for Doc, who never drank alcohol unless a disguise required it.

Pauncho lit up a long green, Cuban cigar and said, 'Doc, the floor is yours.'

He added, 'And the furniture, too, if you so desire.'

Barney groaned. Cobbs and Villiers sat down before Doc could ask them to.

Doc said, 'Did you two have any trouble getting out?'

'No,' Cobbs replied. 'We just walked out the front way. Everything was clear.'

The titian-haired woman shuddered and said, 'All those bodies . . .'

'You didn't tell the police here,' Doc said. 'Obviously you didn't have enough time; you got here so fast.'

Cobbs said they had come straight down the mountain path to the inn. They did not know what was going on and they did not care to know. Their brief interviews with Iwaldi had scared them. The ancient dwarf – the 'mad goblin' – had impressed them deeply. He seemed to be evil incarnate, and they were convinced that even if they had escaped him they would not be safe until they got to England.

'Just what were you digging for?' Doc said.

'Some years ago, when we were here on vacation, we heard about a shepherd who had discovered a stone with some strange markings on it. We investigated and found a rock with inscribed runic signs, made by some Germanic speaker by the name of, by a curious coincidence, Iwaldi. Probably the runes were incised between 600 A.D. and 800 A.D. We sniffed around that area and found a site of a small village. So, every now and then, we dig around here during our vacation. We're on sabbatical leave just now.'

Doc made a mental note to check on their stories.

He could understand their fear. But what they had seen in the labyrinthal tunnels would establish them among the world's greatest archeologists if they were to reveal their discovery. All they had to do was to get the police up there, and Iwaldi would have to run for cover.

On the other hand, they may have reasoned, quite correctly, that Iwaldi had enormous influence and could abort any attempt by the police to get into his castle.

Doc asked a few more questions. Cobbs said that the helicopters which had landed the invaders had left by the time they reached the castle's front door. But he was convinced that some of the invaders had gotten out alive. Apparently, the invaders must have split up, and the second party had survived. He thought so because he had seen the glow of cigarettes far below them on the mountainside path. It was true that the smokers could have been extremely early hikers or maybe forest rangers, but he doubted it.

'I'm asking you to stay here for a while. For today, anyway,' Doc said. 'If any of those invaders are now in the village, you could identify them for me.'

'And what would you do to them?' Cobbs asked.

Doc did not answer. He looked at the young Englishman with all the intensity of his peculiar brass-shot gray-green eyes. Cobbs returned his stare with one just as unabashed though not as intense. Doc had been a practitioner of hypnosis for years and had been able to disturb many a man to the point of hysteria just by looking at him. But Cobbs was a tough and cool character.

Barbara Villiers, who looked devastatingly beautiful despite staying up all night, said, 'I'll stay if you think it'll help you any.'

'Babs!' Cobbs said reproachfully. 'You might at least consider my feelings in this matter. After all, we are engaged! And we agreed that I am the head of the family!'

'There isn't any family yet!'

'Fabulous!' Pauncho said, grinning like a hungry monkey at her.

Cobbs sneered at Pauncho and said, 'Discretion directs me to get out of here now! But I don't want you to think I'm a coward, and if my fiancee insists on behaving foolishly, then I'll stay too. But only long enough to look over the guests here and ascertain if we can identify any as the men we saw in the castle.'

Barney had opened his mouth to say something, then he thought better of it. He looked as if he would explode if he did not get to ask Doc Caliban something at once.

Doc, guessing what he wanted to say, turned away from the couple and winked at Barney. Barney went into the bathroom. Doc said, 'If you'll feel safer, you can sleep here in our beds. We'll make do on the sofa or the floor.'

'I would prefer we do that,' Cobbs said. 'To return to our own rooms now would be stupid. Of course, we have to go there to pack, but we can do that later.'

Doc suddenly spoke to the two in a somewhat musical speech, low-pitched and with many glottal stops and fricatives.

The two only looked startled. Doc spoke in English. 'Your profession hasn't taken you into the Central American jungles, then?'

'No,' Cobbs said. 'What was that for?'

Doc spoke to Pauncho, who listened intently and asked him to repeat several words. He and Barney had only recently learned the speech of the People of the Blue, a dialect of the 'red skinned Athenians of Central America,' and they were a long way from being as fluent in it as their fathers had been. Pauncho nodded and left the room for the lobby downstairs.

Cobbs said, 'Look here! I don't like this mysterious conversation. If you have anything to say, speak English, man! We're not under suspicion, you know!'

'You're not innocent until proved guilty,' Doc said. 'Not in this affair. Everybody is suspect. You are not being detained by force, however. I must insist that you understand that. You may leave at any time you wish.'

Doc removed his jacket and his vest. Barbara Villiers stared and then said, 'I thought you looked awfully fat in the body, yet your face wasn't fat at all. And your friends looked incongruously bulky, too. Good heavens! You must be carrying enough weight in those vests to sink a battleship!'

Doc did not reply.

Cobbs and Villiers went into the large bedroom where he sprawled out on Doc's bed and she on Barney's. Barney came out of the bathroom and spoke softly in the speech of the People of the Blue.

'I sent out a message to Grandrith. His wife answered. She said he'd taken off for Africa a few hours before. She also said she might have to leave her rooms and go hide out in another place. She noticed a couple of suspicious characters hanging around in the street below. She said they might not be interested in her, but she's taking no chances.'

'You told her about the events of the past few hours?'

'Everything. She said she'd pass it on to Grandrith when she got a chance. He's supposed to send her another message as soon as he's ready to leave the plane on the coast of Gabon.' There, near the place where he had been born, Grandrith would proceed on foot through the belt of rain forest stretching over a good part of central Africa. He would live off the plants and the animals native to the land, killing them with arrows or his knife. He would avoid all human habitations; he would go like a shadow, like *the demon of the forest* as so many natives called him. Some used the name that an American writer had given him after accidentally finding out about him. On foot and almost naked, he would go faster than any human should through the silent closed-canopied, twilit rain forest where the only humans are the pygmies and where the pathetically few hairy and long-canined hominids, those beastmen of native legend, not long ago roamed.

Grandrith's wife, Clio, was staying in a slums district of London where she was operating a shortwave radio.

Caliban's cousin, Patricia Wilde, was also in London. She was on the trail of old Anana, the woman who headed the Nine. She believed that Anana lived at least part of the year in a town house in a wealthy residential district, and she was investigating a number of houses there. Caliban did not think she would have any luck, but at least it would keep her busy, and she did have a sharp nose for clues; she would have made an excellent private eye.

The phone rang. Doc was across the room like a bronze shark and had picked up the receiver before the second ring. Pauncho, speaking mainly in the language of the Blue People, said, 'I checked out their registration here, Doc, after greasing the desk clerk's palm. Cobbs and the redhead have been registered here for a week. But the clerk says they aren't round much. I just saw two guys that looked pretty mean to me, like they could take care of themselves and others, too, if they were paid enough. They've been registered here for a week. They're Germans, Heinrich Zelner and Wilhelm Gafustimm. Zelner moves slow and careful, as if he's hurting. They're in room 215. You want – ?'

Caliban asked for a detailed description. Zelner could have been one of the men he saw when he had looked into the room where the invaders were. He might have been wounded during the fighting.

'I'll be right down,' he said. 'Meet you outside their room.'

He checked the pockets of his vest, which had dried out very quickly after he'd come out of the Toll River. He was short of anesthetic gas bombs, so he went into the bathroom and pulled a section of the wall aside. The shortwave radio and their supplies were stored here. Pauncho had cut out a piece of the wall and made a receptacle in less than fifteen minutes after they had moved in. His work on concealing the new door had been so skillful it would be doubtful that anyone would ever know about it until the inn was torn down.

The grenades were actually little plastic balls which shattered easily on impact. Their surface held a little nipple which could be squeezed off and a slender tube could be inserted into the hole created. Doc also took several of the tubes. Cobbs and Villiers seemed to be sleeping. The woman was heart-achingly beautiful.

'You stay here and keep an eye on them,' Caliban said to Barney.

'Why does that *Pan satyrus* always have all the fun?' Barney said, more to himself than to his chief. But this time he was surprised. Doc did answer.

'Pauncho'll be jealous because you'll be with the woman,' he said. 'He'd like the job of guarding her.'

'Some guard! But what good is that going to do me with that Cobbs fish. . . ?'

He stopped talking. Caliban had gone as silently and as swiftly as a wind-blown cloud across the face of the moon.

On the floor below, Pauncho came down the hall with the rolling gait of a gorilla unaccustomed to walking only on its hind legs. He was grinning, and he held a stethoscope device in one huge hairy hand.

'I listened in on them,' he said. 'They didn't talk much but I heard enough. They were up at the castle. They're waiting for orders from someone.'

'We'll find out,' Caliban said. His voice was level, but inwardly he was disturbed. What group could be fighting the Nine? Or was it some group that knew nothing about the Nine but had it in for Iwaldi for some reason? They must really hate him to go in for such overkill tactics.

Doc decided not to transmit the gas via a tube through the keyhole. He knocked on the door and then

Pauncho listened with the sound-amplifier applied to the door. He grinned and whispered, 'They didn't say a word. But I'll bet one signaled the other to cover him while he answers.'

A deep voice spoke in Austrian German. 'Who is it?'

'Telegram, sir,' Doc said in the local dialect and with an adolescent squeak.

'Slip it under the door.'

'Sorry, sir, I can't. It has to be signed for.'

There was a click, and the door swung open a few inches. An eye looked out. Doc seized the knob and jerked the door open with such force that the man was left staring at his hand. He had been holding onto it and had not expected that anybody short of a gorilla could have pulled the knob loose from his grip.

A second later what could have been the hypothetical gorilla charged into him, lifting him up and off his feet and doubling him over a hard shoulder. The man went *whoof!* Doc Caliban came in on Pauncho's tail, struck the man on the jaw as he went by, and then stopped. The other man, a tall skinny fellow with a shock of yellow hair, had stepped out from the bathroom. He held a .38 automatic in one hand.

Doc raised his hands. Pauncho dumped the unconscious man from his shoulder and also lifted his hands. A moment later, the skinny man looked surprised, and he started to open his mouth. Doc caught him as he sagged forward and eased him to the floor. By then, it was safe for him to begin breathing. He had broken two of the gas balls under his feet just as he stopped to raise his hands. It was an old trick that had been working for thirty-five years.

When Zelner and Gafustimm awoke, they were in chairs and their feet and hands were taped and their mouths were gagged. Doc was about to inject Zelner with fluid from a big hypodermic needle.

After he had shot both men in the arm, and they had

gone back to sleep, he removed the gags. His questioning was swift and direct, because he did not know how much time he had. The inn was beginning to stir. Even though the ski season was long gone, there were a number of tourists who had come here to bathe in the mineral waters of Gramzdorf, which were reputed to have medicinal effects. It would be impossible to carry the two men up to Caliban's room without being observed now. And the two obviously expected visitors or a message that had to be answered soon.

The men replied to each question as all men did under the influence of calibanite. But they answered literally and only to the detail specifically required by the inquisitor. Both men told similar stories. They had been hired six years ago in Hamburg. They worked for an organization which they knew was larger than their immediate group. But that was all they knew of it. They had never heard of the Nine nor seen anyone answering to the description of the Nine. Their immediate superior on this job was a scar-faced Prussian known to them as Ruthenius von Zarndirl. He had led them into the castle last night but had disappeared during the fighting. When Zelner was wounded, Gafustimm had been ordered to go with him to the upper levels to route any stragglers while the others went off in two groups after Iwaldi. They had found no one, had returned to the ground floor, waited a while, then come down to Gramzdorf. On the way, they had run into van Zarndirl, who had told them to wait at the inn for instructions.

Doc removed the tapes and ordered them to go to bed. Like zombies, they shambled forward and climbed into their beds. After receiving a shot of a sleep-inducing drug, they began snoring loudly. Doc and Pauncho left the room, and Pauncho hung a DO NOT DISTURB sign on the knob.

They went back up the steps and down the hall to the door of their room. Pauncho rapped out the recognition code on the door with his knuckles. There was no answer.

Doc inserted the *saac* into the keyhole, twisted it as he held one end to an eye, and then quickly withdrew it.

'Barney's on the floor. Lots of blood.' he said.

Pauncho grunted as if a big fist had slammed into his stomach. A second later, he was inside the room with Doc on his heels.

Doc Caliban said, 'Some of the blood is his but most of it is somebody else's.'

The bronze-skinned giant removed a case which looked exactly like a cigarette lighter from a pocket of his vest. He pressed down on the lever, and a humming emanated from it. He passed the device back and forth over Barney's head at a distance of two inches. After a minute, Barney's eyelids fluttered and then his eyes opened. Pauncho had brought a glass of water. Doc popped a pill into Barney's mouth and Pauncho held his head up while Barney drank.

The most serious wound was from a knife that had penetrated a half inch into Barney's shoulder. Instead of sewing up the wound, Doc held the edges of the skin together and sprayed it from a can. The spray dried and solidified quickly, looking just like a piece of Barney's skin. The other two wounds were treated similarly, and then Barney was given another pill. His color returned, and after a while he said he was hungry.

Pauncho complained that his mother did not raise him to be a cook or a bellboy, either. Doc told him to go down to the inn's kitchen and supervise the preparation of breakfast, and never mind if the chef thought he was acting peculiarly.

By then Barney had told his story.

A few minutes after Doc had gone down to the second floor, someone knocked on the door. Barney asked for identification. It identified its owner as Joachim

Minter, chief of the local police.

'What do you want?' Barney said.

'We want to question Mr. Cobbs and Miss Villiers,' Minter replied. 'We have received some information about them from the Ministry.' He did not say what ministry.

'Open up, please!' the voice said sternly.

Barney did not know what to do. To gain time he said that he would wake up the Englishmen and ask them what they wanted to do.

He turned to walk into the bedroom, heard a click, turned again, saw the door open, and three men enter. All three were in police uniform. The chief, a tall man with a big nose and several knife scars along his cheek, said, 'You will please stand aside. Mr. Banks.'

Barney started to protest when one of the policemen struck him on the chin with his fist. But Barney rolled with the punch and countered with a fist in the solar plexus. Then he felt a shock in his shoulder and was dully aware that he had been stabbed.

Barney brought his own switchblade knife out and stabbed the man who had stabbed him. The two grappled. Barney was aware that the pseudochief had gone into the bedroom, but he was too busy to determine what happened after that. He cut up both men but one hit him on the temple with his fist, and that was the last he remembered until he saw Doc above him.

'You were lucky you didn't get your throat cut,' Doc said. 'I suppose they didn't want the hounds called out after them. A corpse might get the authorities aroused.'

'Then Cobbs and Barbara are gone?'

'Gone,' Doc said. 'You feel up to any violent activity yet?'

'I'm shaky, but breakfast will fix that up,' Barney said. 'Why?'

'The men who took them away are doing one of three things. They're holding them someplace in this inn or maybe in the village. Or they're taking them up to the castle. Or they're taking them out of the village to some other place. But I doubt that they'll try to keep them prisoners in the village itself for very long. That'd be too difficult. But they would have to change clothes immediately, because the real police are too well known. So the pseudochief – sounds from your description like von Zarndirl – and his men may be inside the inn yet, changing clothes and arranging for a getaway.

'If von Zarndirl is working for Iwaldi, then the two'll be taken up to the castle. I don't know what value Cobbs and Villiers have for Iwaldi. The fact that he didn't kill them when he caught them in his castle and that he wants them alive now – if von Zarndirl is working for him – shows that they've been holding out on us.'

'You should have used calibanite on Cobbs and Villiers,' Barney said.

'If I get my hands on them again, I will.'

The phone rang. Doc was across the room as if the ringing was a starter's pistol in the hundred yard dash. 'Doc,' Pauncho's bottom-of-the-barrel voice said. 'I just saw three men driving out of the courtyard with Cobbs and Barbara in the back seat!'

'Be right down!' Doc Caliban said. 'Meet us at our car! Bring food; we'll eat on the run!'

Pauncho was standing by the car with a big cardboard box balanced on one huge hand. Doc lifted the hood of the Mercedes-Benz and looked for bombs. Then he slid under and inspected the bottom for explosives or signs of sabotage. Satisfied, he got out from under and into the driver's seat. Barney got into the back seat and Pauncho sat down beside Doc.

There was only one way out of Gramzdorf. Doc drove as swiftly as he could through the narrow streets, which were occupied by enough locals that he had to take it easy. He used his horn when they showed a reluctance to get out of the way. But Gramzdorf was small, and within five minutes they were on the asphalt road which wound up the mountain for many miles and then would begin a descent. Von Zarndirl's car was not in sight yet, even though it had only about five minute's headstart. Doc was driving over the narrow road as if he were on the Indianapolis Speedway. Pauncho ate with a nonchalance that irked Barney, who did not care at all for the depths whizzing by a few inches from him.

'Karlskopf is twenty miles away,' Doc said. 'They can take a private plane from there.'

The sky was blue above them, and the spring sun would be above the mountain across the valley to their right within an hour. But to the west black clouds were advancing. Pauncho stopped stuffing his mouth long enough to turn on the car radio. A German announcer verified the threat of the clouds. A storm was blowing in from France.

Barney moved over to the left side where he did not have to see the abysses springing up at him every time they took a curve. He said, 'Pass some of that wiener-schnitzel or whatever it is back here.'

'Very good stuff,' Pauncho said. He lifted a bottle of dark beer from the box, tore off the cap with his thick teeth, and drank deeply. 'Ah! Nectar!' he burped.

Barney said, 'You're disgusting! What about it, Doc? You want Pauncho to feed you while you're driving?'

Doc shook his head. He did not want to be distracted by anything. Besides, he had just seen the car they were chasing, another Mercedes-Benz far ahead. It was on a higher level and just going around a corner of the mountain. It was moving suicidally fast, too.

The whole affair was puzzling. What group could be fighting the Nine? And why? Who were Cobbs and Villiers? Obviously, they were more than just archeologists on a sabbatical.

Doc drove as if the car had become, in a mystical

manner, a living thing that was also part of him. Even Barney felt this emanation from Doc and relaxed, though he still did not move back to the right.

Then their auto screamed around a curve and there, some fifty yards ahead, blocking the road, was von Zarndirl's car.

'Hey, Doc!' Pauncho said. 'I saw Barbara going up the mountainside! Up in the woods there!'

Caliban could not spare even a glance to look where Pauncho's finger was pointing. He was using the brakes to halt the Mercedes-Benz before the ambushers could fire at close range. He succeeded in stopping the vehicle, though not without some fish-tailing and then backed it up with a roar. The expected gunfire did not materialize.

'What's going on?' Barney said.

Doc gestured with a thumb behind him. He had been looking in the rearview mirror. Barney and Pauncho turned their heads and saw two men coming out of the brush behind them about fifty yards away. One held a rifle; the other was looking down into a metal box he held before him.

Doc started the car forward with a surge that burned rubber and threw the others back against their seats. Brakes and tires screaming, he stopped the car with its nose almost touching the side of von Zarndirl's car. He threw open his door and fell out, was on his feet, and racing around to the other side of the car blocking their path. Von Zarndirl could be in the bushes just above waiting to catch them when they retreated from his aides, but he had to take that chance. He opened the righthand door in the front and looked inside. The keys were still in the ignition lock.

Pauncho, looking in on the other side, said, 'Hey, Doc! Why don't we just drive this – ?'

A crack from up in the hills made him dive to the road. A bullet struck the pavement near him and screamed off. The report of the second shot came almost immediately after.

Doc leaped up, ran to the front of the car, lifted the hood, and then dived back to the pavement by the side of the car. The hood was perforated twice and the windshield once. But Doc was up and looking down over the side of the car at the motor. He rolled away as three more bullets went through the raised hood and through the windshield. Then, fluid bronze, he was back again, had reached in and yanked loose a wire and dived away again.

Pauncho and Barney were firing at the two men far down the road with their automatics. Seeing that the range was too far for accuracy and that the men were not even bothering to fire back, the two stopped shooting.

'What are you doing, Doc?' Pauncho called.

'I just disabled a bomb under the hood,' Caliban said. 'They expected us to drive their car out of the way; we'd have been blown to kingdom come!'

There was a trail up the mountainside. It was visible only in a few places, and in one of these Doc saw Villiers' red hair and Cobbs' black hair for a moment. His gaze kept going up the slope until it stopped on a whitish object. This could be the front of a house perhaps a thousand feet up.

Doc Caliban relayed this information to his men. 'They didn't pick this spot for an ambush just by accident,' he said. 'They've got a place up there!'

If that was true, then the group von Zarndirl represented had planned well ahead. The two men Caliban had questioned probably knew of this place. But they would have said nothing about it unless they had been asked about it. And since Doc did not know about it, he could not have asked about it. Doc swore to present future prisoners with some general questions which might turn up items like this.

'Look out!' Pauncho yelled.

Doc stuck his head up, risking another bullet from the sniper, to see what Pauncho was alarmed about. He did not hear the bullets, but he did hear the two reports coming from somewhere in that mass of evergreens above. And he saw the thirty or so ravens and hawks swooping down the mountainside toward them. They were so close together they almost formed a solid black ball, and they were only a few feet above the tips of the trees. They made no cries, and they bore little white objects on top of their heads.

All three men began firing, then stopped as a dip in the ground took the birds out of their view. The man with the rifle down the road began firing slowly, forcing Pauncho and Barney to get between the two cars and lie flat on the road. The sniper in the trees continued to shoot at Doc. And then the birds, wings beating, beaks open, were on them.

It was impossible to stay out of sight of the two riflemen and fight the birds at the same time. Barney and Pauncho tried; they rolled over on their backs and shot straight up into the feathery avalanche that hurtled on them. Doc hosed the eight ravens and three hawks that came at him with the .15 caliber bullets from his gasgun, and the lead birds exploded in blood, bone, and feathers. But five birds got to him, and he had to drop the gun and defend himself with his bare hands. All of them tried for his head, and in so doing they got in each other's way: wings beating against wings knocked them down, talons extended to sink into his flesh touched another bird and automatically sank and beaks snapping for eyes and nose closed on wings and legs and heads.

Ignoring the sniper because he had to, Doc reared up like a whale coming from the deeps, sending ravens and hawks flying off him. He whirled around and around, his hands chopping out, breaking wings, cracking necks, smashing thin skulls. But one hawk got through and its talons sank into his face. He fell forward and rolled over and over and then began to unhook the agonizing steel-sharp claws from his cheeks. Blood flowed down his face and over his chest as he cast the body of the hawk away from him. He had twisted its head off with one turn of the wrist.

Barney and Pauncho were killing the last of their attackers with their bare hands, too. Like Doc, they were bleeding profusely from deep gashes on their faces.

Doc had two of the plastic tennis-ball-sized gas grenades in a pocket of his coat. He removed them, twisted the pin of one to the left, and pulled it from the ball. Then he stood up, exposing himself to the fire of the sniper in the hills. He threw the ball as hard as he could over the top of his car. It soared in a high arc as the rifleman down the road shot at it. And while he was doing that, Doc, .15 caliber gasgun in one hand and the second grenade in the other, was racing toward the rifleman.

To explode within effective range of its target, the grenades had to travel one hundred yards. The rifleman did not expect the ball to get anywhere near him. Not at first. But he was trying to explode the grenade in the air to make sure it didn't get close enough to make him even uncomfortable. And so Doc was speeding toward him while the magazine of the rifle was being emptied at the ball. When the rifleman realized this, he aimed at Doc. One round was left, and this missed Doc, who had bounded to one side.

Then the grenade blew up before it hit the ground sixty feet from the rifleman and the man with the box. Doc threw the second grenade then, as the rifleman dropped his FN and pulled out his automatic pistol. Doc continued to zigzag, firing with the gasgun. The second grenade struck the ground and bounced high and exploded a few feet above the heads of the two men.

Doc raced in while bullets from the sniper in the hills whee-ed by him or struck the road near him. Then he had picked up the FN, fitted it with a new magazine, stuck two more in his jacket pockets, put the metal box under his arm, and was running back to the car. Even with his heavy hiking shoes and clothes, burdened with a rifle and a metal control box, and on a tarred road, he was running swiftly enough to have breathed down the neck of an Olympic dasher.

When he reached the cars, Barney and Pauncho were in the one that had blocked them, and Barney had the motor going. Caliban dived into the back seat – Pauncho had left the door open – and the car backed up, stopped with a screech, and then screamed away down the road and around the curve of the hill while bullets struck the car or the road nearby.

About three hundred yards down the road, Barney pulled the car off onto the side of the road, where a stone fence had been erected to keep sightseers from falling off the edge. There were also a little stone restroom and two wooden picnic tables there. Doc gave quick first aid to everybody, himself last. They popped blood-building pills into their mouths and felt the pseudoskin he had sprayed over their wounds.

'Almost as good as new,' Barney said, but he was exaggerating.

The blood-building pills, however, had to be taken with food to do much good. They ate the rest of the breakfast that Pauncho had brought along, even though their appetites were gone. The fight had shaken the two up, and Doc, though he looked calm enough, did not down his food with any pleasure. The pills would send their temperature up by a degree for half an hour and make them feel a little woozy. But their lost blood would have been replaced.

Caliban said, 'Von Zarndirl will've arranged matters

for us in Karlskopf. At least, I'm presuming he will have. Another ambush might not find us so lucky. Besides, I'm not going to bypass that house; it may contain the key to this puzzling affair.'

Barney felt his shoulder and winced a little bit. Doc said, 'You up to climbing that mountain and maybe mixing it up with those baboons?'

'You know I am, Doc,' Barney said. He took the FN rifle held out by Caliban.

Doc Caliban untaped the six sticks of dynamite from the chassis next to the motor, saying, 'We might use these.'

'Hoist them on their own petard!' Pauncho rumbled. 'I like that!'

They crossed the road and began climbing. The woods were heavy with firs and pines, but the underbrush had not begun to leaf out yet. Within an hour they were on top of the ridge on which the house rested. This was about half a mile to the south. From there on they proceeded even more cautiously because there was always the chance of mines or ambushers. Doc went on ahead to allow his puffing and panting compatriots to get their strength back. He saw the white house through the trees a hundred yards away from it. He also detected the gray slice of a partly hidden wire stretched across the path that wandered up from the road. He went around the tree to which one end of the wire was fixed and approached within twenty feet of the rear of the house. It was a one-story frame house with a big stone fireplace at the north end, the end near which he crouched. It was built in the form of an L and had about four narrow windows on each side. The blinds were pulled down almost to the bottom of the windows.

He returned to his men. 'There's no sign of life,' he said, 'but you can bet they're all in there, waiting. Of course, they don't know we've come up here, but they can't afford to ignore the possibility.'

Each of them had two of the bouncing gas grenades, the last of their supply. Doc said, 'Let's go,' and he seemed to the others to have dissolved into the forest. Pauncho said, 'Don't foul things up in your usual slap-happy manner, Barney. Try to keep from falling over your own feet.'

'You low-browed hairy monstrosity!' Barney said. 'I hope you can keep from swinging from the trees; they must really be tempting you! Keep your mind on our business and don't shoot me by accident!'

Pauncho grinned and said, 'It wouldn't be any accident.'

They saluted each other with fingers to noses and, still grinning, slipped into the woods. Barney went east, below the house, and cut across the path. Though he was not the equal of Caliban in moving swiftly and quietly through a forest, he was superior to most men. His rapier form moved past naked-branched bushes and over twigs with not a sound. Pauncho, even though he went much more slowly, made more noise. He cut to the west on the back side of the ridge and far enough below the house to make sure he wasn't seen. Then he worked his way up to the south end.

There was a silence for a long time. Only the faint cries of ravens and the skreek of a hawk disturbed the air. The sun reached the zenith and began to slide down the blue steps. The storm that had been in the west showed no signs of coming closer; it seemed to have run into a wall.

Doc waited. He studied the windows for signs of life, but the thick curtains and the lack of light inside the house hid any faces looking from under the blinds. He was sure that armed men waited there. They had probably called for help; helicopters might appear at any time. The machines that had been used in the attack against Iwaldi could not be too far away. He could not wait until night or until they got so tense that they sent men out to poke around.

Doc cupped his hands close to his mouth and gave the cry of the lark native to these mountains. A few seconds later, the call was answered. Perhaps the men inside the house were fooled, but Doc knew that Barney was returning his signal.

He wormed between the little fir plank outhouse and a small log house from which came the odor of birds of prey.

The piles of lumber and firewood there made for good cover. That would have occurred to the men in the house, too, and they would be keeping a bright eye on the piles.

A third cry of the lark came. This was even less convincing than Barney's.

Doc wormed along the ground until he came behind the outhouse, and he stood up. He could see the limestone chimney on the north easily enough. He stepped back, estimated the distance and the wind again, and tossed the gas grenade underhanded. It flew up in a high arc and came down almost in its target, the square hole on top of the chimney.

It struck the edge, however, bounced up and down onto the sloping roof, bounded along and leaped from the roof's edge and fell onto the ground just below a window. Doc had stepped behind the outhouse by then and put his fingers on his ears. The blast was still getting echoes from the mountain behind him and across the valley when he tossed his second grenade. This disappeared down the chimney and exploded before it reached the bottom. At least, it should have done so. He had sent it higher than the first so that the six-second interval between pulling the pin and the mingling of gases would result in a blast halfway down the stone shaft.

There was the chance that Cobbs and Villiers might

get hurt, but they would certainly be hurt if their captors got clean away with them. They would have to take chances, too. They were adults who knew very well what the consequences of this game might be if they lost.

The echoes of the second explosion had just died when a third, Barney's, blew up just outside the front porch – if Barney had thrown accurately. Doc charged toward the house just as Pauncho's grenade, thrown from the south, blew up the side porch.

Doc was hoping that the rapid succession of blasts would stun the defenders and yet would not kill the prisoners. He ran with the bundle of dynamite sticks held by a cord in one hand. He threw it ahead of him so it landed on the roof, leaped up, grabbed the edge, and swung himself up with the agility of a leopard. An automatic rifle began firing immediately afterwards, and the muzzle, stuck from the window, tried to follow him up. But it was too late.

Somebody began to shoot through the roof. The bullets did penetrate the three-inch thick planks, but he had moved on to a station just beside the chimney. When the firing ceased, he yelled down the shaft.

'Come on out with your hands behind your necks! Or I'll drop this dynamite down the chimney!'

'If you do, you'll kill Cobbs and the girl!' a man shouted.

Doc said, 'So what?'

There was a pause. He resisted the temptation to put his head over the mouth of the chimney to hear what they were saying. Somebody might be down there waiting to shoot his face off.

'O.K.!' the same voice shouted. 'We know when we're licked! We'll come out with our hands up!'

'Send the prisoners out first!'

There was another pause. Then the man said, 'Here they come!'

A banging as of the front door being violently opened announced the exit of somebody. He could not see who it was, but Barney suddenly stuck his head out from behind a tree and signaled. Cobbs and Villiers were being released. A few seconds later, he saw them walking toward Barney, who was waving an arm at them. They looked disheveled, dusty, and a little bloody. Their hands were tied behind them.

Two men came out of the back, three through the front door, and two through the hole blown in the south side of the house by Barney's grenade. They came out shooting wildly. Cobbs and Villiers threw themselves on the ground, but von Zarndirl's men did not care to waste bullets on them. They wanted to get Doc and his men first.

Doc, knowing that some of them would turn and shoot at him, tossed the bundle of dynamite toward the rear door to panic them. Then he leaped past the chimney and down to the ground, landing on both feet but going forward to the ground and rolling. His massive muscles and thick bones enabled him to take the shock without injury. He came up onto his feet, his gasgun spewing at the men in the front, two of whom had run to the north so they could get him in their line of fire. His little bullets ran across their chests, sending up gouts of flesh and blood.

Barney's FN had cut the third man almost in half.

The men in the back had taken off when the dynamite fell near them. They did not know that it had no fuse. They kept on running and so were caught in Pauncho's gasgun fire.

The two men who had gone out through the hole in the south side had been wounded in the legs by Pauncho's first few bullets. One got to his elbows and started to shoot, and Pauncho had to kill him. The other man put up his hands, though he was unable to stand up when Pauncho ordered him to.

Barney had untied the hands of Cobbs and the redhead. She did not look so beautiful now what with the dust and the blood and the grayish skin. But, seeing Doc, she smiled, and at that moment, disheveled and shocked or not, she was beautiful.

Pauncho came around from the side of the house dragging a man along behind him, by the jacket collar. He dropped him before Doc, and said, 'We're in luck! Von Zarndirl, if those scars mean anything!'

Caliban gathered together the metal box and the weapons, and Pauncho dragged von Zarndirl into the house. It was necessary to give him three of the blood-building pills. There was food in the house, and the German ate after the initial effects of the pills had energized and deshocked him. Doc put Barney on guard outside with orders to watch especially for helicopters. There was a transceiver by which they could have called for help. It had been on a table near the fireplace, and it and the operator lay in two heaps on the floor. Doc's grenade had blown out the upper part of the fireplace, and the stone fragments had shattered the radio and driven a sharp piece into the operator's neck.

The interior of the house was a mess. Shattered glass, ripped blinds, curtains, overturned tables, and pieces of stone and dust lay over the single big room.

Doc injected calibanite into the arm of von Zarndirl. Within fifteen minutes he had cleared up some of the mystery.

Von Zarndirl was working for an organization which had to be the Nine, though he did not know what its name was or even that it had a name.

Doc's face did not show it, but he was shocked. Even though he and Grandrith had turned against the Nine, he had never thought about others doing so. And Iwaldi himself was one of the Nine who sat at the table of power.

70

Von Zarndirl was too far down in the echelon of the Nine to be a 'candidate'. He did not know that Iwaldi was one of the millennia-old rulers of the organization for which he worked as cutthroat or whatever job was required of him. All he knew was that orders had come through to get the white-bearded old dwarf, Graf von Gramz. Von Zarndirl was lucky. He had led his group upstairs and lost some men to wolves and owls, and then he had gone down to the ground level to look for the other group. They had found a concealed entrance to the underground passages, but this was not the one which the first group had gone through. (Von Zarndirl did not know this, of course, but his description told Caliban that he had missed the obvious trail. How he had managed to do this, Caliban could not know. He supposed that the man had simply found an entrance before he had gotten to that left open by Caliban.)

Almost immediately, three-fourths of the group had been crushed against the wall by a sliding stone block. Van Zarndirl, in the lead, had escaped by an inch. The survivors, five men, had refused to go on. Von Zarndirl had returned to Gramzdorf (the choppers having departed long before by prearrangement), and he had reported via radio to a Herr Schmidt, whom he had never seen. His men had observed Caliban's group, but whoever it was that received the report did not recognize any of them. Or if he did, he did not tell von Zarndirl their identities. Schmidt ordered that Cobbs or Villiers be taken for questioning. The old Norwegian, Sigurdsson, and his two companions were to be kept under close observation. If a chance arose, they were to be taken alive. But if they looked as if they might get away, they were to be killed.

Doc Caliban was puzzled. Schmidt knew that the two Englishmen were somehow connected to the old Norwegian (Doc Caliban) and his cronies. But what of it? Unless Schmidt knew that Caliban was in

Gramzdorf in disguise, he would have no reason to suspect Cobbs or Villiers. He did not know that they had been Iwaldi's prisoners or that Caliban had helped them escape. Although von Zarndirl's men had seen the two Englishmen go to Caliban's room, that would not mean anything.

And if any of the servants of the Nine had suspected that Sigurdsson was really Caliban, von Zarndirl would have been ordered to attack Caliban without thought of consequences. Cut him down in public, in front of the police station and a hundred witnesses if you have to! We'll get you off later, you can be assured of that. And you'll never have to work again or want for anything, short of a seat at the table of the Nine.

His disguise had not been penetrated. But he had been gone from the inn during the night of the attack, and that may have been what aroused suspicion.

He asked von Zarndirl if this were true. The scarfaced German, sitting on a chair, staring glassily straight ahead, replied in a hollow voice. He did not know. One man had been left behind to observe the village during the attack and to warn the attackers if the villagers became aware of what was going on at the *schloss*. He had reported the disappearance of the Norwegian and his companions. Von Zarndirl had passed this information on.

And Cobbs and Villiers had disappeared for three days. Anything out of the ordinary, anything unexplained, was to be reported.

He continued to question von Zarndirl. Yes, he supposed that the next time many more men would be used. Yes, he did not think it likely that Iwaldi would remain in the castle now, but such decisions were not up to him. If they were to attack an empty castle, they would do so. Whatever his boss, Schmidt, ordered, they would do.

Doc took one of the plastic hemispheres from a

pocket and showed it to von Zarndirl. He asked him a few questions and received answers which confirmed his guesses.

The metal box and the plastic hemispheres were developments of devices Caliban had been working on when he had gone mad from the side effects of the elixir. The hemisphere housed electronic microcircuits which were connected to the brain of an animal through tiny holes drilled into the skull. The electrodes were inserted into those areas of the brain controlling specific behavior and also were connected with the visual neural system. The hemisphere transmitted a line-of-sight beam of what the animal saw to the transceiver of the metal box. This had a screen which displayed a picture of everything that came within the animal's vision. This was fine in the case of sharp-eyed birds, but the images were often fuzzy in the case of dogs or other near-sighted animals.

An animal or a group of animals could be roughly controlled by moving dials on the face of the control box. An animal could be driven to attack by stimulating the part of the brain which controlled aggression. But if it saw two persons before it, and the operator wanted it to attack only one, the animal was likely to attack both anyway. A fast operator could alternate states of aggressiveness and of fear very swiftly in the animal and so crudely stimulate or inhibit its attacks when it was confronted by more than one person.

The screen of the control box was also capable of producing up to twenty different simultaneous views, and a skilled operator could control that many individually, though not to the degree wished. Or the operator could control the entire group as one.

Doc Caliban had been close to finishing his proto-type just before he went insane. After he had turned against the Nine, their agents had taken over his laboratory in the Empire State Building and his research facilities in his estate near Lake George. They had studied all his notes and the plans for many devices which he had perfected but had not yet released for use by the Nine.

Doc Caliban had guessed all this when the wolves had attacked him in the bedroom of the castle. Iwaldi had – or once had – his own animals, and the others of the Nine had theirs. Doc wondered where the man who had directed the wolves first and then the birds in Iwaldi's castle had been stationed. Of course, though the transmission was only on a direct line-of-sight and very limited range basis, the beams could be detected by transceivers and transmitted by wire to remote control posts.

Doc Caliban asked von Zarndirl what frequency his group used when directing their animals. The German did not know. This did not disturb Caliban, because he would examine the control box himself.

Barney came into the door – after calling out that he was entering – and said, 'A chopper's coming. There may be more than one. It's hard to tell. The storm must be coming closer, too.'

Doc Caliban looked out the window. The grayish-black western skies had broken loose from whatever was restraining them. The ominous clouds were spreading eastwards as if chased by furies.

He saw the flash of sunlight in the air above the distant peak just before the sun was veiled by the clouds. Then he saw three tiny objects.

He turned and said, 'Let's get out of here. Pauncho, you take care of von Zarndirl.'

Pauncho said, 'What do you mean, take care of him, Doc? Bring him along or shoot him?'

'Bring him along. He's of no use to us anymore, but. . .'

This was a war in which no rules of humanity applied. Or had been applied. But Caliban was getting increasingly reluctant to kill his enemies in cold blood. It was one thing to kill during combat. But to shoot a helpless prisoner was another thing. Not that he had not done that nor that Barney and Pauncho had not. When Doc was only seventeen and a lieutenant in World War I, he had captured two German soldiers at the same time that he had been cut off by the advance of the enemy. It had been necessary for him to get back to his own lines and yet he could not do so with the burden of the two prisoners. He could turn them loose or tie them up and leave them. While he was trying to make up his mind, he was joined by a captain and two sergeants, also cut off.

The captain had said that he was sorry, but they could not take the prisoners back. It would be too risky; they would be lucky to rejoin their forces without the burden of the prisoners. And it would not do to release two men who would soon be shooting at them again. The captain ordered the prisoners shot.

Doc had told the captain that he should perform the execution himself. If he couldn't do it himself, he should not ask his men to do so. The captain became furious and threatened Caliban with a court martial when they returned. Caliban replied that he had not disobeyed an order. He had merely stated an opinion. Besides, he doubted that the generals would permit such a charge to be made. The last thing they wanted was the civilian populace to know that such deeds were not rare. It did not matter that the French, British, Italian, Turkish, and German armies were all doing this under similar circumstances or even when there was no good reason.

The captain ordered Lt. Caliban to shoot the prisoners.

Caliban had never forgotten the faces of the two Germans. One, a tall brown-haired man with a black stubble of beard, had not said a word. He had glared at Caliban and then spat at him.

The other, probably even younger than Caliban, was a slight tow-headed man with greenish eyes. He had tried to be brave but, as Caliban raised his pistol, he had fallen to his knees and begged for mercy. The .45 in his chest knocked him backward into the mud. The other German, screaming his hate, rushed Caliban with his bare hands. Caliban shot him in the forehead and stepped aside to let the body, carried by the charge, slide on its face down a slope and into a shellhole full of water.

'There,' Caliban had said to Captain Wheeler. 'I have done the job you weren't man enough to do.'

Wheeler was white with rage, but he said nothing. They started to sneak through the German lines. Caliban halted suddenly, and, for one of three times only in his life – that he remembered – wept. He sobbed for ten minutes and then continued on his way. When he was close to the American lines, he was shot at. The bullets were close, but he got away and then came up on the would-be killer from behind. The man was Captain Wheeler.

Caliban took his automatic away from him. Wheeler said he would charge Caliban with trying to murder him. Caliban said he did not think so, since a dead man could not bring charges. He stuck Wheeler's face into the mud and held it there until Wheeler quit breathing.

That was when he first met Barney's and Pauncho's fathers. Rivers was a colonel then and Simmons was a major. (Both were to be promoted shortly after.) They had been captured by three soldiers but had escaped. They came up just in time to see Wheeler try to murder Caliban and his execution afterward. At first, they were hostile, even though they knew that Caliban had been provoked.

He explained exactly what had happened, expecting to be put under arrest. But these two were not the dyedin-the-wool military type; they were highly unconventional, and both had gotten into trouble because of some of their antics and their outspokenness. They told him to forget it, that Wheeler had it coming. As for the shooting of the prisoners, that had been necessary and it was doubtful that the sergeants would report it. Or, if they did, that their report would get very far.

Rivers (Barney's father) got Caliban attached to his staff. He recognized even then the genius of this young giant. In the few months that Caliban remained in the infantry (his true age was discovered and he was discharged), Caliban came to dominate the two older men. Or, perhaps, it would be better to say that he fascinated them.

Caliban kept in touch with the two after the war. He went to Harvard (Rivers' school) and graduated in two years. He had never competed in athletics because it would not be fair, and he did not want the publicity to interfere with his studies. Even though he was capable of getting through medical school (Johns Hopkins) with the highest grades in two years, he had to take the normal amount of time. But he had plenty of opportunity to study many other subjects than those required, and his friendship with many professors enabled him to use the laboratories. In 1926, he completed his internship, but he had the equivalent of several Ph.D's in widely separated fields. And he continued his studies in them and took up new subjects even while he was practicing brain surgery.

In 1927, the Nine made their first contact with him. In 1928, he was formally invited to join, and in 1929 he first attended the grisly and horrifying ceremonies in the caves of the Nine in east central Africa. But he was now immortal, barring accident, suicide, or homicide. His life would end by homicide if he did not obey the Nine in everything they ordered – he was assured of that. In matters which did not concern them, he could do exactly as he pleased. He could carry on his battle against crime as he wished, could perform brain operations on criminals to eliminate their compulsive antisocial attitudes. There were, he found out, times when he had fought and eliminated certain great criminals who were servants of the Nine and, in two cases, candidates. But the Nine had not seen fit to interfere with him since he was not interfering with any of their projects at that time.

Caliban's father had trained him from infancy to be a superman dedicated to fighting evil. Of course, if his son had not had the potentiality, he could not have developed into a superman no matter how much training he had had. But Caliban's heritage would have made him the greatest athlete of the modern world – except for one – even if his childhood had been normal. His grandfather had been one of the Nine. XauXaz had been born about 10,000 years ago – or more. And XauXaz's father had been born about 40,000 B.C. (here Caliban was speculating), so that old XauXaz was actually one of those Old Stone Age men whose massive skeleton and muscles made them much stronger than the strongest of modern man. Moreover, there was some evidence that XauXaz and his two brothers had been contributing their genes for a long, long time to the family which eventually became known as Grandrith.

Caliban's father, a candidate of the Nine, had gone mad from the side effects of the elixir in 1888. He had become that infamous murderer, Jack the Ripper, for a short period, and then, recovering his senses, had fled to the States. But not before fathering James Cloamby, the future Lord Grandrith, known also by The Folk as *tls* and in the human world by the anglicized name his 'biographer' had given him.

Caliban's father had been so horrified by what he had done when insane that he had sworn to make amends. He had raised his second son as a deadly weapon of retribution against evil. And this extreme physical and mental and moral education had resulted in a superman.

But you get nothing without paying for it, Caliban thought.

The universe was a check and balance system from macrocosmos through microcosmos. Man, intermediate in size between the two, atom and the star, but the most complex of all objects, is no exception. James Caliban had paid. His high ideals and his high goals had resulted in too much self-control. Too much inhibition. And, admit it, a feeling of superiority, no matter how carefully he hid that feeling from others and, worse, from himself. That superiority – which did exist – had alienated him in many respects.

A stranger in a world he had never made; his father had made it.

And his father had intended to turn him against the Nine eventually, he was certain of that. His father must have blamed the Nine for that period of murderous insanity and for the price they sometimes exacted for their immortality. His father had prepared him not only to fight the obvious criminals of the world. He had secretly waited for the day when he would launch him against the Nine.

But the Nine had offered the elixir to the son before the father could reveal his plans. Caliban, who prided himself on his invulnerable morality, had said yes to evil when offered a chance to live for 30,000 years. His father had not known that, any more than Caliban had known that his father was also a candidate. Neither had ever attended the ceremonies at the same time, and neither had had reason to tell the other that he was a candidate.

And so the Nine had found out that his father was planning treason. Or his father had failed the Nine in some way. And they had killed him. Caliban had no proof of that, but he was sure that they had. The circumstances of his death were such that only the Nine would have been responsible.

Caliban had tracked down his father's murderers, but these had not known that they were working for the Nine. And the man who had transmitted the orders from the higher-ups had died without revealing that he was not the originator of the murder.

It was his father's death that had caused Caliban to devote himself wholly to the fight against evil – except where the Nine decreed otherwise. The lust for immortality had made him schizophrenic. He knew that now. He had known it then, but he had pushed that knowledge down into the mass of his unconscious.

He had gathered around him men who were highly knowledgable and multiskilled and who had a thirst for adventure. Rivers and Simmons and Williams and Shorthans and Kidfast. He had met the other three a few months before he was discharged. He had kept contact with them while at Harvard and Hopkins, met them now and then. His father became good friends with them, and they sorrowed almost as much as Doc when his father died. It was then that they had accepted his invitation to join him in his crusades, and the first thing they had done was to help him run down his father's murderers. And –

'Doc! Hey, Doc!' Pauncho growled. 'What's the matter, Doc?'

Caliban shook his head and blinked. He said, 'I was thinking. . . .'

'The choppers are coming fast,' Barney said.

Caliban went out swiftly with the others behind him, Pauncho behind von Zarndirl, guiding the somnambulist with a word now and then. They went down the path for fifty yards and then cut into the woods, the cars their destination. Doc returned up the slope and climbed up a fir as agilely as a young gorilla.

One of the choppers settled down in the space north of the house, and men carrying rifles scrambled out. Another landed near it; more men got out. Then a man carrying a black box got out and turned some knobs. About twenty hawks flew out of a port of the second chopper. They spread out in all directions, two flying toward his area. He dropped from branch to branch swiftly and fell the last twenty feet to the ground.

The party was still making its way down the mountain toward the road. Doc Caliban caught up with them, appearing so suddenly that Cobbs and Villiers jumped.

'Give me the box,' Doc said. Von Zarndirl handed it to him, and he quickly checked out the operations of the controls, all of which were marked with their functions. The power gauge indicated that the battery was almost discharged, and he had no other.

There was a flutter above a tree to their right. They moved backward to crowd behind a tree, but Doc did not think that the hawk would miss them. The dial had been set at a frequency which he supposed was the one being used when the original operator had dropped the box. He adjusted two dials beneath the four-inch square screen, and then pointed the red arrow marked on the center of the upper edge of the top of the box at the bird.

One of the disadvantages of this was that the beam between animal and box was tight. A fast moving bird was hard to keep track of. This device, however, bore a dial which moved to indicate the direction in which the animal had moved when the beam lost contact with it. Also, it continued to move in the same general direction of the target if the operator pressed a button. This activated a broadcast pulse which triggered off a mechanism in the hemisphere, and the operator, by moving the box and noting the swing of the needle, could narrow down the area in which the target was.

Then it was up to him to catch the tight beam again.

An operator needed lengthy training to be skilled. Doc Caliban, after a minute of experimenting, acted as if he had been through the required courses. But he had an advantage in that he had originated the theory of the TV-controlled animal.

The whiteness of the screen was suddenly a green and black picture – no color-blindness in a hawk – of branches and the ground seen between the branches sliding by swiftly. And then there was a bronzed face down by a tree. Other faces and parts of bodies. The hawk had spotted them and was coming toward them.

Doc looked up from the screen, saw the wide wings spread out stiffly as it sailed between two trees, and he said, 'Get him, Barney!'

The FN banged three times. The hawk flew apart under the impact of at least two bullets.

Doc pulled out his handydandy, a combination knife, corkscrew, screwdriver, crescent wrench, and you-name-it. He quickly unscrewed the four screws holding the instrument panel to the box and ran his gaze over the circuits. It would have taken him much time to ascertain the function of each if he had not designed the prototype himself. He pried up four connections and exchanged them, and then said, 'Down to the cars! I'll be behind you!'

The chutter of a helicopter became louder. They retreated under several bushes and stayed motionless while the craft circled around and around near them. Suddenly, a hawk flying at near top speed flew over them, turned, and shot back. But it had spied the dead hawk on the ground. It flew around and around until the chopper nudged it away and hovered over the spot.

'They know we're close!' Pauncho said.

Doc did not reply. He had moved the box around and now had zeroed in on the hawk. He pressed a button, and the hawk, zigzagging crazily, flew off. But it returned a moment later on a straight course.

'I set up the circuit to trigger its fear center,' Doc said. 'There isn't any button on this particular instrument panel for that, but the circuits can be arranged to stimulate fear if the button is pushed.'

The hawk circled again, apparently again under control by the enemy. The copter moved toward them with rifle and heavy machine gun barrels sticking out of the ports. Doc pressed the button again, and the hawk wheeled swiftly and ran head-on into the nose of the craft. It bounced off and fell suddenly into a tree.

Doc spoke to Barney while still looking at the screen as he moved the box to try to pick up another bird. 'Move slowly. Give me a grenade.'

Barney extracted a pressed-down grenade from a big pocket in his vest. It expanded to its tennis ball size as he opened his fist to hand it over. Caliban slowly squatted down, laid the box on the ground, and took the grenade. He waited for the chopper to come close enough so that the men in it could discern them under the bushes. Pauncho and Barney had readied their FN's. Doc Caliban said, 'Save your ammunition unless I miss. We'll need all we have if the other choppers come after us.'

But the chopper swung away westward. They got away as fast they could at an angle down the mountainside. The roar of a chopper was suddenly on them, and then, a moment later, a wind struck the forest. It was the storm.

Lightning veined the dark eye of the sky. Thunder cannonaded. The chopper dipped as the first fist of the wind struck it. It went on over the two cars parked on the other side of the road, swung out over the valley, rose straight up, and then beat a path against the increasing wind back up the mountain slope.

The air whistled through the limbs of the trees, which thrashed like the arms of men trying to keep warm. Pauncho yelled, 'Good thing that storm hit when it did! They must have known we were here when they saw those cars! Anyway, they would've landed and checked out the registration and then they wouldn't have stopped till they found us!'

'Why always tell us the obvious?' Barney howled. He and Pauncho grinned at each other, happy because the storm had saved them.

Doc told the others they should wait until it got even darker or until rain came. Though the choppers were probably being tied down in the clearing by the house, men might have been sent up into a tree to survey the road. And if they saw the two cars driving away, they might send a chopper out after them, wind or no wind.

In ten minutes the rain came down half-frozen. The black asphalted road became grayish white with the first drops and then black as the drops melted. They left the woods and got into the cars. Doc ordered that they return to Gramzdorf, since that was the last thing that the enemy would expect them to do. Their rooms were still available, since they had not cancelled them.

Doc drove his own car with Carlos Cobbs and Barbara Villiers as passengers. He was silent for half the journey back and then he said, 'Are you up to going with us tonight?'

'Where are you going?' Cobbs said.

'I intend to get into Iwaldi's place again. I could find the place where you two fell in when you were digging, but it would be quicker if you pointed it out for me.'

'I'll be glad to!' Cobbs said. He lit up an American cigarette. 'I owe that insane goblin a debt. But I still don't know why you don't just call in the authorities.'

'They would just come in and look around and then depart without doing a thing,' Doc said. 'Unless we had some evidence that they could not overlook. You can bet that Iwaldi has cleaned up the mess in the castle and buried the bodies some place. And you can bet that he would bring pressure to bear in the highest political circles to keep the police out. What must be done will be done by us.'

'Or by this organization that von Zarndirl belongs to?'

'They may try again tonight, storm or no,' Doc said.

The car rocked with the wind's buffets. The half-rain, half-snow splopped on the windshield and was carved away by the wipers. Doc was driving at about fifteen miles an hour because of the limited visibility and the wetness of the road.

'I don't want to be left behind just because I'm a woman,' Barbara said.

'The invitation included you.'

He turned on the headlights.

She patted Caliban's huge arm and said, 'I like your trusting a frail vessel such as myself.'

Doc flicked a sidewise look at her but he did not reply. She had not shown the slightest sign of fear or hysteria, and outside the house she had picked up an automatic rifle and checked it out as if she were a veteran soldier.

He drove for several miles more in silence, wondering why they did not ask more questions. He was taking a chance by bringing them along if they were agents for the Nine. They might get an opportunity to trip him up. But if he left them at the village, he would not be able to keep his eye on them.

The storm continued for hours after they got back to the inn in Gramzdorf. Cobbs and Villiers went to their rooms. Barney immediately set up the radio in the bathroom. The contact man in Paris reported that no word from Lady Grandrith had been received. But he did have a message from Lord Grandrith. It had been sent by an operator for the Nine while Grandrith held a gun to his head.

Grandrith's communications, as usual, were more

than cut to the bone. They went all the way to the marrow. He had been met by a big party of men out to kill him, and he had eluded them so far. He would be going on, as planned, on foot. It was doubtful that Caliban would hear from him again for several months. Caliban wished that Grandrith had added more details. Then he smiled slightly. His half-brother was no more taciturn than he was. Both talked as little as possible. But his brother did so because he had been raised in the jungle with sentients who did not converse much after they became adults. And he had spent much time with himself during the formative years. Grandrith's close-mouthedness was 'natural.' Caliban's was the result of his father's training and was 'artificial.' And also 'neurotic.' There were times when it was clearly to everyone's benefit to talk much, and he found it difficult to do so then. He did, however, talk vicariously through the pseudo-hateful banter of Barney and Pauncho, as he had done with their fathers. Though their insults sometimes irritated him, he needed the two men.

Von Zarndirl, having received another injection, slept on Doc's bed. Pauncho brought up more food from the kitchen after observing its preparation. He grinned as he told about the curious looks that the chefs gave him and how he had pacified a waiter with a huge tip.

'They think we're crazy, and of course they're talking about us. Half the village must know we're acting very peculiarly.'

'We'll move out at nine o'clock,' Doc said. 'According to Cobbs, the cave-in is only two miles from here, on the north side of the mountain and about 2,000 feet below the castle.'

At nine o'clock the storm had been dead for an hour. The wind was gentle but icy; the clouds were ragged, passing below the moon slowly as if they were battle-torn veterans on parade.

Von Zarndirl, taped and gagged, slept on the floor of

the bathroom. The others, bundled up in climbing clothes, carrying alpenstocks and various boxes, went out a side door of the inn. They tromped through the slushy streets to where they had left the cars. After examining them for booby traps, they opened the doors and got out their rifles. They put on the caps with the blacklight projectors and their goggles and began tramping up the mountain, Cobbs leading. Water fell on them as they passed under the low branches of trees or by bushes. The earth was often slippery under them, but they dug in with their stocks and slogged on up.

Cobbs stopped for a moment and said, 'It's about a quarter mile ahead.'

'We'll go more cautiously now,' Doc Caliban said. 'Iwaldi is no dummy. He'll have back-tracked after he caught you and either shut up the entrance or stationed a guard there.'

They started walking again. The moon came out. Doc, looking up, saw the first of the big winged shapes. The broad beam from the projector revealed *lammergeiers*, the eagles of the Alps. There seemed to be dozens, and all were heading toward them.

He said, 'Look out above!' and shifted the metal box he had been carrying on a strap around his shoulder to a position on his chest. 'Don't fire!' he said. He pressed a button on the top of the box and held it there.

None of the humans could hear the noise that was broadcast from the box, but the eagles turned and flapped away swiftly to escape the eardrum-paining frequencies.

Immediately after, Barney said, 'Doc! Wolves!'

Doc looked up and saw the first of the big beasts bounding over a bush to their left. But it was not a wolf. It was a large blackish German shepherd dog. Behind him came three more and behind them six big Doberman pinschers. Their mouths were open, revealing their sharp teeth, but they uttered no sounds.

A few minutes later, they turned and bounded away as if they had seen a pack of tigers.

Doc and his party climbed on toward the excavation, taking advantage of every bit of cover. The eagles and the dogs would undoubtedly be back. The noise had momentarily overcome the stimulus of the micro-current in the hostility area of their brain. But once they were out of the influence of the supersonic frequencies, they would return.

'How can they see us, Doc?' Pauncho said. 'I mean, how can the operators of the control boxes see much through the eyes of the animals in this dark?'

'I doubt they're using TV tonight,' he said. 'It's too hard to keep the narrow beams locked in under these conditions. They probably are just transmitting the code that turns on the juice to the aggression areas of the brain and letting the animals attack whatever they come across.'

'I hope so, Doc,' Pauncho said. 'If they can spot us through the eyes of the birds, we're going to have a hard time.'

'Here they come again,' Caliban said. He had turned the sound generator off so that the animals would not be affected until they got close.

The eagles, their only noise the flapping of their wings, and the dogs, their only noise the brushing aside of the wet rain-covered plants, came in swiftly. They had but one intention: to tear apart these strangers in the dark.

Then Doc pressed the button, and the dogs whirled so fast they slipped in the mud and fell on their sides or scrabbled desperately to keep from sliding on down the slope. The eagles veered away and were swallowed by the night.

A minute later, the birds and the dogs were charging in again.

Thirty seconds later, they were frenziedly trying to get away from the invisible agony.

'How long's this going on, Doc?'

'Until something – or somebody – breaks,' Caliban said.

Pauncho knew it was useless to ask him to elaborate.

The next time, the birds came in first and the dogs did not appear until the birds had been turned away.

'They're catching on,' Barney muttered.

'And probably moving in on us,' Pauncho said.

'Isn't it really too risky to stay in this one spot?' Cobbs said. 'I think we should be moving about a bit.'

'That's up to you,' Doc said. He pressed the button again as the first of the birds appeared. This time they kept on coming and had almost reached them, with Doc saying, 'Hold your fire!' when they broke and flew upward.

The dogs bounded down the slope again, just as the birds turned away. Doc said, 'Hold your fire on these, too, unless you can stick your guns down their throats.'

'The whites of their eyes, heh, only closer yet? Pauncho said.

Some of the dogs slipped in the mud and slid into them. The others turned away just before the final leaps and went crashing into or over the bushes and down the hill.

Three dogs hurtled in, sidewise or fangs first, and Pauncho and Barney slammed one each over the head or the back and then kicked them on down the hill. Cobbs and Villiers hit a dog at the same time with the barrel of their rifles, breaking its ribs.

Doc said, 'It ought to be over soon, one way or the other.'

'What makes them voiceless?' Pauncho said. 'I looked in the neck of a bird with its throat cut open back at the house on the mountain, and its vocal cords were all there.'

'I saw you,' Doc said. 'But I supposed you'd guessed the answer. There are a number of electrodes at various areas of the brain. During the time that the animal is released for attack, its voice centers are inhibited.'

'I wondered about that,' Cobbs said. 'But things have been happening so fast, I didn't have time to ask about it.'

'I just supposed their vocal cords had been cut,' Barbara said.

The others did not comment. Pauncho had asked Doc about the lack of voice after the attack by the wolves in the castle and Doc had given his opinion. But after the attack of the birds at the house on the mountain, he had told his colleagues not to mention anything about the characteristics of the animals. He had wanted to determine if the English couple would be curious about the strange lack of cries from the animals. If they did not comment, they might refrain because they knew the reason.

On the other hand, it was true that events had come one after the other and might have distracted them. But Barbara seemed to be a very stable and self-possessed person, and Cobbs, though he showed some apprehension, was far from hysterical.

The birds came first and the surviving dogs, going much slower because they had to climb uphill in muddy earth, attacked simultaneously. This time the wings of the eagles beat so close that the tips of some touched their faces. But the birds swerved again and shot back overhead. The dogs turned tail when they were still a few feet from closing with the party.

'I'd think they'd go crazy,' Barney said. 'They're being pulled apart by the opposing drives.'

'They may yet,' Doc answered.

About two minutes later the birds came in again, and this time Caliban turned off the sound generator for a few seconds after they had wheeled around to go in the other direction. The dogs then had nothing to stop them except the weapons of the party. While the others knocked the dogs on the head as they struggled uphill to get at them, Doc Caliban pressed a button on the other box, which had been on the ground by him. He had rearranged its circuits so that the aggressive areas of the brains would be stimulated.

The others did not notice what he was doing since they were concentrating on smashing in the dogs' skulls or backbones and doing a good job of it. He had not told them his plan, since he never confided to anyone unless he needed cooperation.

There were yells and screams to the right up the mountain, and then rifles and pistols banged away. Doc indulged himself with a broad smile. The others had their backs turned and would not be able to see him.

He switched off the aggression transmitter and turned on the sound generator. The two surviving dogs leaped backward down the hill as if they had stepped on a red-hot plate. One turned over and kept on sliding. The other regained his feet and fled.

'What's going on, Doc?' Pauncho said, jerking a thumb in the direction of the gunfire.

'As soon as the birds were deflected again, and presumably heading back toward the men who'd launched them, I switched off the noise generator and turned the aggression stimulation on. The birds, of course, attacked the first living things they saw, which were our enemies.'

'Fabulous!' Pauncho rumbled. 'I wish I had one of those hemispheres stuck on Barney's head. Then I could keep him from making a monkey of himself.'

'Since when does a monkey's uncle know anything about proper behavior?' Barney said.

'The conflict of noise generator versus aggression stimulation might have driven them mad, anyway,' Doc said. He led the way toward the groanings and whimperings drifting ghostily through the bushes. Approaching cautiously, they found six men on the ground, all alive but three totally unconscious and the others semi-conscious. The birds were all dead, since they had not ceased to attack until killed. The onslaught had been so unexpected that none of the men had had time, or opportunity, to turn off the aggression stimulator. The birds had tried for the face and the throat and had blinded four. One man died of a ripped jugular vein while Doc was examining him.

After giving the survivors a shot to ensure that they would be unconscious for a long time, the party picked up some more magazines for their rifles and stuffed them in their capacious pockets. Pauncho and Barney threw the extra rifles down the mountain, and they continued climbing. They did not have far to go. Cobbs stopped suddenly, grunted, and said, 'There it is.'

In the blacklight of their projectors they could see the trenches that the two archeologists had dug.

'Where's the cave-in?' Pauncho said.

'It's not there any more,' Barbara Villiers said.

Doc began to poke his alpenstock into the bottoms of the trenches but stopped. He had heard the far-off chutter of helicopter vanes. He resumed probing and then said, 'It's been walled up.'

'Where'd those men come from?' Villiers said.

Doc did not reply. He took from a side pocket of his vest a tiny instrument and, holding it in his hand, began to walk back and forth for twenty yards each way. He worked his way up the mountain while she wondered aloud what he was doing. Since neither of his colleagues were sure, they did not answer her.

Ten minutes later, Caliban reappeared so suddenly from behind a tree that Barbara jumped and Cobbs wheeled around swiftly, bringing his rifle up.

Doc stepped back behind the tree and said, 'Don't shoot.'

'Doc, you shouldn't do that,' Cobbs said. 'You're likely to get shot.'

Caliban said, 'Follow me.'

He led them upward to the right for about twenty yards and stopped. They were facing a fairly smooth outcropping of rock. Doc Caliban walked forward on the apron of the rock extending from its base and pushed on a small boulder at one side. The boulder rocked; there was a grinding noise and a section of the outcropping slid to one side.

'How'd you find it, Doc?' Pauncho said.

Doc tapped at the pocket which now held the small device he had used when casting back and forth. 'It indicates small changes in the local magnetic fields. It detected the hollow behind that rock, and so I looked for something that would be the entrance activator.'

They went into the chamber which had been cut out of the solid granite. Doc pulled a lever sticking out of a box in a corner, and the ponderous section of rock slid back into place. Immediately after, electric light bulbs fixed to brackets about four feet from the floor, and about thirty feet from each other, lit up. These were connected to wires which, in turn, occasionally descended the wall to the generator on the floor. Doc recognized the foot-square metal boxes as his own invention. They stored electricity derived by amplification of the flux of the earth's magnetic lines of force. They could not provide much current for very long, but the bulbs probably did not get much use in these corridors. They became extinguished as soon as the last person passed them, and they lit up as soon as the first person got within ten feet of them.

Each one in the party held his rifle across his belly. Doc held his with one hand while the other was extended with the magnetic-field discriminator.

Whenever it was a question of going to left or right, Doc looked at the juncture of floor and wall. Cobbs had carefully made tiny markings with a pen the first time he had come here. These indicated their previous route so that they would be able to find their way out.

They went up steps cut out of stone to upper levels four times before Cobbs finally called a halt.

'We're getting close to the place where the dwarf captured us.'

They were standing in a round chamber about forty feet across. It contained a dozen large boxes of oak on which were carved hunting and battle scenes. The costumes of the dwarfs and the humans in the scenes were those worn circa 800-900 A.D.

'They look like coffins,' Pauncho said to the woman.

'They are coffins,' she said.

She tried to raise a lid but could not manage it. 'It's so heavy,' she said. 'But you should see the mummified body and the jewelry and gold it's decorated with.'

'Here, let me help you!' Barney and Pauncho said. They collided with each other in their eagerness to get to the coffin.

'Leave it alone!' Doc said. 'They might be booby-trapped now!'

But Pauncho, grinning because he had shoved Barney out of the way, had started to raise the lid. Barney dived for the floor as if he expected the coffin to explode. Barbara gave a small scream. Pauncho had stepped back and dropped the lid, which was raised about eight inches. It did not drop. Instead, it continued to rise, and the figure in it sat up. He held an automatic pistol in one hand.

At the same time, the lids of the other coffins screeched upward, and other figures sat up aiming automatic pistols at them.

A voice behind them said, 'Freeze!' A voice ahead of them said, 'Not a move!'

'A beauty of a trap!' Pauncho whispered. He looked at Doc Caliban. The huge man was obeying instructions. He had no choice. The fire from three sides would have cut them all down within a few seconds.

Ten minutes later, their hands cuffed behind them, they went up stone steps onto another level. The twenty men who accompanied them kept pistols pressed against their backs. They marched down a long tunnel on the walls of which were hung many paintings done in a very primitive but forceful manner. It looked as if this were the place Iwaldi had chosen as his ancestral gallery. The paintings were mainly of long-bearded fierce-faced men with beetling brows, bushy eyebrows, round blobs of noses, and very broad shoulders.

Doc Caliban remembered, however, that Iwaldi had been born long before portrait painting of this sort was known. These dwarfs must be men who had inhabited this underground fortress; perhaps they were Iwaldi's descendants, not his grandsires.

Except for the paintings, the tunnel was bare rock.

They were marched into a square chamber and here all the prisoners were forced to undress. The inspection that followed was thorough and included probing for concealed objects. Doc's wig and facial pseudoskin was pulled off. Two false teeth containing explosives and a coil of very thin wire were removed from his mouth.

Barbara Villiers said nothing. She was as dignified as if she were wearing a formal at the opera. Out of regard for her, Barney and Pauncho repressed the ribald comments they would have made at each other's expense.

They were marched into a chamber about fifty feet square. Stone steps cut into the sides of the walls led up to three levels of runways carved out of the rock. A man led the way up on to the second level. Just past the nearest of many entrances was a room divided by two sections of thick iron bars. The man opened a door set in the first by inserting a thin metal rod into a hole and pressing a button on the rod. The door swung back, and the party was marched up to the next section of iron bars. This was opened in the same manner, and Caliban, van Veelar, and Banks were locked behind it. But Barbara Villiers and Carlos Cobbs were left outside. The men conducted them out onto the overhanging runway and around the corner. An iron door clanged. The men marched away. Presumably, the English couple had been locked in a cell facing the runway.

'I wonder why they separated us?' Pauncho said.

Doc did not answer.

Days passed. At least, it seemed that many days passed. They had no way of determining time except by the number of meals, and they got so hungry in between these that they were sure many were being skipped. They exercised and slept and talked much, though when they did not want to be understood they talked in the language of the People of the Blue.

The only person they saw was the man who brought their meals, and he never said a word.

Then, three or four or five days after they were captured, two men entered the outside cage. Both were walking backward and holding a box with a short antenna directed at the beast which shambled around the corner. Two men came behind the animal, one of whom also held a box with an antenna directed at the beast.

This was a huge grizzly, the North American *Ursus horribilis*. Its head swung low, and its eyes were a bright red. Its open mouth dripped saliva.

The man with the box in front backed up to the wall, keeping his antenna pointed at the grizzly's head. Then he pressed a button, and the grizzly lay down and went to sleep.

The great head was only three feet from the prisoners, who could see the tiny hemisphere on top of it.

The two men got out of the cell quickly and closed the door with a loud clang. The grizzly quivered at the sound but continued sleeping.

One of the men holding a box pointed it at the beast, and, suddenly, the ponderous animal was on its feet and roaring. It reared upon its hind legs and advanced toward the prisoners as if it intended to go through the bars to get them. The man pressed another button, and the beast dropped to all fours. It no longer seemed angry; it was just curious as it prowled around the cell, sniffing here and there and stopping for some time to gaze at the prisoners.

Barney said, 'Do you think Iwaldi intends to let that bear loose on us?'

Doc Caliban called loudly, 'Mr. Cobbs! Miss Villiers! Can you hear me!'

Cobbs' voice was faint but distinct. 'Yeah, I can hear you!'

'Just testing!' Doc Caliban said. 'Can you see anything of note?'

'Just some of Iwaldi's men! Nothing of Iwaldi!'

A moment later, 'Correction! Here comes Iwaldi!'

Doc Caliban looked through the double set of bars but did not see the old dwarf appear as he had expected. About ten minutes afterward, the long-bearded hunched figure appeared from the right. Evidently, he had come up steps to the right instead of taking the closer steps to the left.

The grizzly roared on seeing him and pressed against the bars as if it were trying to get its muzzle through and bite him.

Two boxes with antennae were pointed at the bear,

which immediately backed away and stayed in a corner while Iwaldi and four men entered. Two kept their antennae directed at the grizzly, during the conversation that followed.

Iwaldi rolled forward like a sailor, his body hunched forward and his arms swinging at his sides. His long white hair fell to his shoulders and his white beard swung like bleached Spanish moss in a wind. The wrinkled face came close to the bars but not so close that Doc Caliban could reach through and grab him.

Iwaldi stood for two minutes staring at them while his thin lips slowly opened into a wide smile. The eyes were as red as the grizzly's.

Finally, the thin and cracked voice spoke.

'You'll not get out of this, Doctor Caliban!'

'And why not, ancient fossil?' Caliban replied evenly.

Iwaldi cackled. 'Do you think that you, a baby, a born-just-yesterday, could anger me with your puerile words? So I'm a fossil? Well in a way, you're right, since fossils endure while flesh dies. And you'll die, Caliban, and soon! Very soon!'

Doc Caliban shrugged and said, 'Maybe I will. Since you think I am going to die, it wouldn't hurt you to tell me what's going on. Are you and the Nine really at war? Or did I make a bad guess?'

Iwaldi fingered his beard with a deeply seamed and swollen-veined hand for a minute. Then he said, 'It can't hurt to indulge an ephemera such as yourself. And the knowledge might make your end even less endurable to you.

'Yes, Old Anana and her sycophants are at war with me! But it was I who declared war, not them! I almost got Anana and Shaumbim and Ing! We were to meet in Paris, and I arranged to have the walls of the house loaded with explosives! I was to arrive a few minutes late to the meeting, just after the smoke cleared away!

98

But that Anana! She hasn't survived for over 30,000 years by being insensitive. She smelled death in that house! That's the only way I can account for it! She sniffed out the odor of coming death! And she left the house and took Shaumbim and Ing with her and was only a block away when the house blew up!

'She should have blamed you or Grandrith for that, since she knows you're capable of doing that! But the fact that I was late made her suspicious, and she sent me word to come to a house in London. She did not say why, but I knew. I was to be put on trial! Iwaldi! On trial!

'I sent her a letter impregnated with chemicals which would release a poison gas when the envelope was opened! But she had someone else open it, and that person died, of course! From then on, it has been a battle! I finally decided to hole up here in my ancient stronghold, this mountain that was the property of some of my ancestors, the kings of the southern branch of the Gbabuld family! But I'm getting out now – for the time being – and leaving you here to face whatever you must! And whatever you must will be a matter of choice! So thank me for giving you a choice of deaths, Caliban!'

'Why the war at all?' Caliban said, ignoring the reference to deaths.

'Because the others have opposed me! They have sided with Anana! I wanted to let the mortals poison themselves and so eliminate themselves in time! I wanted to permit pollution to continue, the air to be fouled, the waters to be fouled, the fish to die, the ocean plants to die, the trees to die! In a few years, most of mankind will be dying of starvation! You know that! You said so in your report to us in 1946. You extrapolated almost one hundred percent what would happen, what is happening now and what will happen! You stated that enough people would become alarmed that measures would be taken to combat pollution! But it would be too late! The politicians would take over the fight against pollution and use it for their own advancement! And most measures would be band-aids whereas deep excisions and grafts were required! Those were your own words!

'So, in about twenty years from now, a flicker of an eyelid in my lifetime, mortal, the sea life will be dying and there will be the very good chance that the world's oxygen supply will be seriously reduced.

'I wanted the Nine to keep their hands off! Let the mortals kill themselves off! Not that all of them would die, which is a pity, though it would be nice to have servants. But so many would die that civilization would collapse, and then the planet could begin the process of cleansing itself. Once again, we'd have pure air and pure water and trees would cover the land and the animals would return in great numbers. And we could set ourselves up as gods, as we did in the old days, and this time ensure that the mortals stayed few in numbers and poor in science. We wouldn't make the same mistake all over again of letting them multiply and invent until suddenly the entire Earth was threatened!

'But Anana said no. She said that if we let them go, we might die, too. The whole Earth might die. Only the most primitive forms of life would survive.

'I said that we had the means to restore the proper balance when we wished. Your report said that your own researchers had come up with a means whereby the phytoplankton balance could be restored and the chief source of the world's oxygen would thrive again. We could use that after the mortals had become savages again and the cities were being uprooted by the plants and being buried under the good earth.

'But they overruled me. Anana said that we could not afford to take a chance. We did not want to die, too, though she admitted that the prospect of a return to the good old days was tempting. She is very, very old, as you know, Caliban, but she remembers when the great forests covered Europe and even the isles of Greece were green with trees. She remembers when North Africa was wet and verdant. She remembers when you could travel for days in what is now France and not encounter a single human being. She remembers the great and the small beasts that lived in the forests.

'But she decided that we would not let things take their course as determined by the mortals. She said that we must start using our influence on the governments to determine the effective course in fighting pollution. Action had to be taken now, and we would start planning our campaign immediately. Not for the sake of you ephemerae, you know that. But for the sake of the blessed green Earth. And for our sake.

'So I appeared to agree, and I left. But Anana found out that I was secretly preparing countermeasures, and she summoned me to that house in Paris. And I set the trap, and it failed. But I will win. Old Iwaldi won't fail! Although you won't be around to witness my victory!'

'And that is the only reason why you have deserted the ancient table of the Nine?' Caliban said.

Iwaldi stared for a moment and then said, 'Is that *all*? What do you mean?'

'There isn't some other reason you haven't told me?'

Iwaldi laughed so hard he had to bend over, and his beard almost touched the floor. When he managed to straighten up, he wiped the tears from his bloodshot eyes with the tip of his beard, and he said, 'You're very clever, indeed, mortal! Very perceptive! It is too bad . . . if I could trust you . . . if only . . . but no, I can't! Yes, there is another reason, but even though you are to die, I won't tell you that! It'll give me some pleasure to know that you'll be wondering what that other reason is up to the moment that you start suffering so much you'll have no thought for anything but the pain!'

'Does this other reason have something to do with the English couple?'

'Why do you ask that?'

'Because they must have some value to you, otherwise you would have killed them the first time you had them. It would be easy to find out if they were spies for Anana by injecting calibanite. And once you found out, you would kill them whether they were innocent or guilty.'

Iwaldi made a smacking sound and said, 'Very well reasoned out! You are indeed a worthy descendant of mine!'

It was Caliban's turn to be surprised, but he did not betray it with any change of expression. He said, 'I know that XauXaz was my ancestor and I had suspected that his brothers were, too. But I did not suspect . . .'

'The Grandrith family tree has more than one god in its branches,' Iwaldi said. 'Even Anana was one of your ancestors, though she provided a son a long time ago, about the time the primitive Germanic speech was starting to split up into its North, West, and East branches. Which means that you have none of her genes, of course. But her sons became heroes of their people. They were as strong as you or your half-brother. But I was your great-grandfather, Doctor Caliban, though my genes seem to have been most prominent in another branch of your family, not in your direct heritage. Didn't you know that Simmons, your colleague, was my grandson? Haven't you thought about his extreme shortness, his massive trunk, his abnormally long arms and short legs? His Neanderthalish supraorbital ridges? All of which characteristics, except for his height, have been inherited by his son, Mr. Van Veelar, doomed to die with you also. Then there is another illustrious descendant of mine, a second cousin of yours and of Simmons, a scientist who brought back some rather strange specimens from a high plateau in South America in the early part of this century. He also looked much like me.'

'Cousin George Edward!' Caliban said.

'Grandpa!' Pauncho said, sinking to one knee and spreading his arms out wide. 'Grandpa!'

Iwaldi stared at him and then smiled thinly.

'Very well! Clown away to the last minute! Very admirable! I wouldn't like to think that my great-grandson was a coward, though it doesn't really matter.'

'And you'd kill your own flesh and blood?' Pauncho said, rising.

'Why not? It wouldn't be the first time. An ephemeral is an ephemeral.'

A man appeared at the outside bars. The grizzly growled but did not move from the corner. The man said, 'Pardon, sir, but the invaders are getting closer. They'll soon be on the third level.'

Iwaldi said, 'In a moment the servants of the Nine will find out they will have to keep on going down. A river of flame will appear behind them. Napalm is being forced by pumps into the tunnels. They'll try to take tunnels leading away but will find their route barred by big blocks of stone. They'll be herded, as it were, down to this level.

'In the meantime, I've opened a vein of water, and the tunnels below this are filling with water. They'll flood this level – unless the river of napalm gets here first. It'll be quite a race between the two, and if you prefer drowning to burning to death, you had better start praying.'

He stopped. Caliban, van Veelar, and Banks returned his gaze. He said, 'I like spirit in a man except when it's turned against me, and even then it affords me a challenge, however brief – a break from the boredom of mundane life. Do you see that?'

He pointed at a metal box protruding from the corner of the ceiling and the right wall.

'That's a movie camera. It will record your last moments, and then the front end will be automatically covered by a metal plate. When I return, I'll recover it and run off the film. It'll be a pleasure to review your deaths.'

He gestured at the two men with the boxes directed at the grizzly. They stepped backward, and the men with the rifles followed them. Iwaldi walked backward for a few steps, too.

'I've made a little arrangement here. Possibly even given you a chance to escape from this cell, though I don't really think so. But if you should get out, Caliban, you will then only have the choice of throwing yourself into the flames or into the water. You can't get past them.'

He turned and walked through the outer door, which a man clanged shut. The grizzly roared and charged the men behind the bars. They flinched, but Iwaldi did not move back, though the grizzly's paw was slashing the air only a few inches from his face. He said something, and the men with the boxes turned the antennae toward the bear again. He sat down and became quite docile. Iwaldi spoke loudly.

'Caliban, at any time you wish, you can slide your door aside and enter the cell with the bear! But the moment you move that door, a mechanism will radiate a frequency which will cause the bear to become insane with a desire to kill. Nor can you all go through the door and then shut it with the hopes that the grizzly won't attack you once the stimulus is removed. That frequency will keep operating even if the door is shut again.

'This outer door can be opened by you, if you can get to it. But it won't open immediately when you pull on it.

A delay mechanism will keep it closed until five minutes have passed after pressure is applied. Which means that two of you can't keep the bear occupied while one opens the door and then all of you escape. The bear will be driven with the desire to kill every living thing in sight. He's nine and a half feet long and weighs one thousand one hundred and twenty pounds.

'You can stay in your cell and wait to be burned or drowned. Or you can fight your way out, and then be burned or drowned, but you'll have a choice. And this time, you'll have nothing but your bare hands and feet, Caliban! Use them well!'

He was silent for a moment as he stared at them and, doubtless, was hoping for a reaction of some sort. But the three were stony-faced.

'I'm going now,' Iwaldi said. 'It can't hurt to tell you that I'll be in Stonehenge for the winter solstice to attend XauXaz's funeral!'

Doc Caliban was surprised when he heard this, but he did not show it.

'Yes, XauXaz's funeral!' Iwaldi snarled. 'You didn't know that, did you! His body has been kept in a big box in a London warehouse. It'll be shipped to Salisbury and then taken to the ruins of Stonehenge, where the Nine will hold the funeral ceremonies for him! And I'll be there, though uninvited! I'll kill all of them! Old Anana! Ing! All of them!

'And then I'll be free to release my biobomb! While the mortals are starving to death and also gasping for oxygen, I'll be in my mountain retreat, snug and safe, eating well, breathing a rich air! After it's over for the mortals, then I and a few of my servants, mostly female, and my stock of beasts and plants, will come out!

'What do you think of that?'

The prisoners continued to stare without expression.

'You can pretend to be unconcerned!' he shouted.

'But you are naked, and I can see your hearts thumping! A long goodnight to you, mortals!'

He spat and walked away, two men preceding him, the others trailing.

Pauncho broke the long silence. 'Maybe the invaders will take pity on us.'

'Yeah,' Barney said. 'They might shoot us. At that, they'd be doing us a favor.'

Pauncho looked at Doc and said, 'I didn't know we were related. That makes me several cuts superior to this proletarian peasant, heh, Doc? I got the blood of English nobility in my veins, right? And the blood of ancient Viking sea kings. And what's more, the blood of men and women that were once gods and goddesses to the common herd, lowly swine like Barney. Say, Doc, what about that hero stuff? Who do you think were those ancient Germanic heroes he was talking about?'

'I don't know. Maybe the men whose exploits formed the basis of the *Volsunga* and *Nibelungenlied* epics. Or maybe the man or men who were the originals of the *Beowulf* stories. I'm more concerned about his descendants, three in particular.'

Pauncho's small eyes widened. 'Three?'

'Yes. That man's descendants have to include most of the present populace of north Europe or anybody descended from north Europeans and probably from south Europeans, and many Africans and Asiatics, too. Figure it out mathematically, if you ever get a chance.'

Barney haw-hawed but quit when the grizzly, roaring, hurled himself against the bars.

Doc said, 'Iwaldi didn't say whether or not pressure has to be maintained on that door. We can't afford to take a chance, so one man should keep pulling on it.'

'If I had a pocket, I'd pull out a coin and we could flip it to see who's the lucky guy,' Pauncho said. 'But I'll be magnanimous, Barney. I'll handle the door while you help Doc with the bear.'

106

Pauncho's voice was steady and he was grinning, but his reddish skin had turned pale.

'No,' Caliban said firmly. 'We'd be stupid to reduce our strength by one-third. We either put the grizzly out of commission and then open the door – provided Iwaldi wasn't lying to us – or we don't make it at all.'

'Well, Barney, you always said you might be skinny but you could lick your weight in wildcats,' Pauncho said. 'Here's your chance to prove it.'

'I said cats not bears,' Barney replied. 'Anyway, the three of us total about seven hundred and seventy so that gives the grizzly an edge of three hundred and fifty pounds. And he's got teeth and claws a hell of a lot sharper than ours.'

'Tell me something I don't know,' Pauncho said. 'Like how're we going to take him?'

He pressed his blobbish nose against a bar and stared at the grizzly. It was pacing back and forth, its head low and swinging, the brownish silver-tipped fur beautiful but the beauty lost on the watcher. There was fat under that loose glossy hide but there were also giant bones and the strength of two gorillas.

'I want you two to hang back in here until I give the word to join me,' Doc Caliban said. 'I'm going to make him chase me until he gets tired.'

Barney and Pauncho looked at the cell, forty feet square, and they said, at the same time, 'Chase you?'

'It's worth a try,' Caliban said. For him, that was equivalent to a long speech by Hector urging the discouraged Trojans to venture out against the Achaeans again.

He pulled back on the door and slipped through. The grizzly bellowed and whirled around, glared at Caliban, and then charged. It went so swiftly that it was a blur to Pauncho and Barney.

But the reddish-brown golden-tinted skin and dark auburn metallic-looking hair of Doc Caliban was a blur, too. He sprang to one side just before the grizzly was on him, ran at the wall, and bounced off it like a handball.

The grizzly rammed head-on into the bars with a crash that shook the bars and quivered the iron floor under the feet of the two men. But the enormous and clumsy-looking beast recovered swiftly, whirled, and was after Caliban, who had sped to the corner where the wall and the outside barred wall met. Again, he leaped to one side, and again the beast crashed with wall-quivering impact.

'If that grizzly's smart, and he doesn't look dumb,' Barney said, 'he'll be watching for Doc's sidewise maneuver.'

'Yeah, but his thinking processes may be overwhelmed by the aggression stimulation,' Pauncho said. 'It may make him all fury and no brains at all.'

The third time, Doc startled his aides by suddenly running at the bear just after it had started its charge. Events happened so swiftly that they looked as if they were being run by a speeded-up projector. The bronze blur and the brownish silver-tipped blur met. But Doc had leaped up and leveled out, and his legs shot out. His bare feet struck the grizzly on the nose and the sides of the head. The two bulks stopped. Doc fell backward but rolled and landed on his side and then was up and away. The bear, roaring, shook his head, while blood flowed from his nostrils, and launched himself at Caliban. The man did not quite succeed in escaping untouched. Claws, backed by a great paw swinging with strength enough to remove a man's head, barely nicked the back of his right leg. The skin came off in a wide band across the back of his calf, and blood ran down his leg.

Caliban spun and ran straight into the bear. The grizzly heaved himself up, coming up off all fours like a killer whale bursting from the sea's surface, and opened his front legs to receive the foolhardy human.

Doc Caliban went on in as if he had lost his desire to live.

Pauncho and Barney cried out, 'Doc!' and Pauncho yanked at the door to pull it back. He and Barney would go out there now; surely this was the time.

But Doc had planted a blow with his huge fist with all the power of his left arm and his back and legs. The arm sank into the fur of the animal's belly, into the fat, and into the muscle.

The grizzly went, '*Oof*,' and it fell backwards.

Doc Caliban leaped back, then, but even as it fell the grizzly's left paw raked the top of Caliban's head, and blood gushed out from a torn scalp.

Doc was momentarily blinded. He turned and ran, judging the distance to the wall by memory, stopped there three paces away, and turned. He wiped away the blood from his eyes, but more flowed down.

The grizzly had gotten to all fours and stood for a minute while it sucked in air. Its belly heaved, and its tongue dangled far out.

Then it charged, more slowly than it had before but still fast enough to have kept pace with many Olympic dashers.

Doc waited until it was very close and then, putting his feet against the wall behind as a springboard, dived under the beast.

It was completely taken by surprise by this maneuver. It whirled around but Caliban had gone between its legs, come up behind it, and was on its back. He seized its ears as it reared up on its hind legs and whirled around and around as if it could catch the man clinging to its back.

Pauncho and Barney, knowing that it would roll over in a minute and crush Caliban, went through the door. Yelling, their hands waving, they charged the bear. It roared and batted at them as it kept on dancing with its partner in his strange position on its back. They danced, too, around the perimeter described by its long claws. Once, the tip of a claw caught the end of Barney's long slender nose, and blood squirted out. A second later, he slipped in the blood which had spilled on the floor from Caliban's wounds and the nose of the bear. The grizzly was so close that it could have dropped on all fours and covered him, but it whirled away.

Doc's hand stabbed out and plucked the hemisphere from its head.

Pauncho lifted up Barney, who was half-stunned when the back of his head had hit the metal floor. Then Pauncho, looking something like a bear with the mange, charged the grizzly. He came diving in just as the animal was half-turned away, and his three hundred and twenty pounds slammed into the side of the bear's right leg.

The grizzly toppled over on its side, which was just what Caliban did not want. But he hung on to the ears and then bent his body back, his muscles cracking with the effort, and tore the ears of the grizzly off with a sound like the ripping of a sail under an overwhelming wind.

The beast bellowed so loudly that it half-deafened the three men. It spun around, and its jaws clamped down on Caliban's leg as he was trying to crawl away through a pool of blood.

Doc, instead of continuing to try to get away, twisted around and brought both fists down hard on the grizzly's skull. And then he hammered the big wet bloody nose with his fists.

The twisting around resulted in great pain and more loss of blood. It was so painful, he felt faint. The grizzly, if it had been able to seize him then, might have finished him in a few seconds.

But Pauncho, roaring, landed up in the air and came down with both feet on the back of the grizzly's massive neck. The impact of those feet, driven by those two extremely powerful legs, stunned the creature, even if only for a very short time. Its jaws opened enough for Doc to pull his leg loose. He rolled away but without his customary speed. Barney, imitating Pauncho's example, leaped into the air and came down on the bear's back. He did not have the weight nor the strength of his partner, but he did the bear some damage.

It coughed and then got to its feet slowly. Blood was running from its nose, from the places where the ears had been, and its eyes were crossed. It stood for a minute, looking at Doc Caliban, who was now crawling away, leaving a red trail.

Pauncho came up from behind the grizzly and kicked him beneath the tail with his right foot. The bear was turned into a maniac again by the kick. It whirled so swiftly that it caught Pauncho by surprise. He tried to run away, but it charged and grabbed him with both its front paws. Pauncho went down screaming under the bear.

Barney, yelling, leaped upon the huge shaggy back and, his legs clamped around the body, dug his thumbs into the eyes. The grizzly, bellowing, released Pauncho and reared up on its hind legs and then fell back, apparently by design, to crush Barney.

Barney fell off and rolled away but not before a paw, batting blindly, scraped his left leg from the top of the thigh to the knee. His blood mingled with Caliban's and the bear's on the floor.

Barney was slight compared to Caliban or van Veelar, but he had a wiry strength that had surprised many a large man who had tackled him. His hands were slender, even delicate looking, but he could double a steel poker. And his hands were strong enough to have dug into the sockets of the skull and popped out the bear's eyes. These were now hanging from the nerve cables on its cheeks.

It was blind, but it could smell, though not efficiently because of the damage to its nose; and it could hear, though not efficiently, because of the pain from the tearing off of its ears. But it located Caliban and went after him, ignoring the others. Doc, hearing the warning cries, turned and got to his feet, though not without difficulty and not without gritting his teeth to suppress a groan.

The bear charged straight into him. Doc reached out and jerked the eyes loose and cast them on the floor and then, as he went down under the beast, rammed his arm all the way into the bear's mouth. It choked, and its paws tore at his back, and then it backed away swiftly. Its jaws opened, to get rid of the object that was strangling it, and Doc's hand came out, closed on the huge wet tongue. The slipperiness almost balked him, but he managed to keep his grip. Only one other man in the world could have done what he did.

When the tongue came out by the roots, the grizzly shot blood all over Caliban and the wall of the room. And then it turned and charged blindly across the floor until it rammed its head into the bars of the inner door. It collapsed there, wailing until blood choked it and it died.

But Doc Caliban had lost much skin and his back muscles were so torn up they were causing him intense pain.

Doc sat up and waved Barney's helping hand away. 'Open the door!' he said. 'We have to get out of here!'

Pauncho was there before Barney. He pulled the sliding door back and said, 'No five minute wait.'

Doc Caliban tried to get to his feet, but he slipped twice. Barney, standing by his side, made no move to help him because he did not think that Doc would like it. It was Doc who always helped others; he never needed anybody else.

Doc wiped the blood from his forehead, looked at Barney with the yellow-flecked verdigris eyes, and said, 'You too weak to assist me?'

'Hell, no, Doc, glad to do it!'

Barney leaned down and let Doc put a massive arm around his shoulder and then he straightened up. Doc came up slowly but not with the full weight of his three hundred plus pounds on Barney's slim shoulder.

'Now I'm up, I can make it by myself,' Doc said. Then he clamped his teeth and pressed his lips together.

'I think I hear something!' Pauncho said. 'Yeah! And I smell something! Smoke! Hey, there's somebody down that way!'

He pointed to the left.

'The invaders,' Doc said. 'Anana's men. Driven here by the flowing napalm, I suppose. We'd better go the other way. Barney, check on Cobbs and Villiers. I don't think they're still here, but . . .'

When Barney returned he said, 'Not there. And there's nothing we can use for a weapon. I didn't see our stuff either. You'd think Iwaldi wouldn't have bothered to hide it, since he didn't figure we'd even get out of the cell.'

'He knew it wasn't impossible for us to get out,' Caliban replied. 'But he must have figured we'd never get out of the cave even if we somehow got past the bear.'

They went down the runway to the nearest stone steps on the right and descended to the floor of the chamber. There were a number of exits. Doc picked the middle central one, and they went down a tunnel. Smoke was pouring out of several of the entrances behind them, and Doc could hear, faintly, coughing from one. They went down the tunnel and came to a shaft which contained no ladder. Caliban, looking down it, saw ankle-deep water on the floor of the tunnel under the shaft. It was rising swiftly.

'This is the tunnel we came up after being captured,' he said. 'It should still hold Cobbs' marks, unless Iwaldi rubbed them out. We'll have to chance that; it's our only hope.'

Slowly, because he felt weak and because the movements pained him considerably, he let himself down the shaft and dropped. The impact almost made him faint. His colleagues dropped down, too, and they went toward the direction which – he hoped – was the right way. The lights along the tunnel were still on but might soon go out. However, since this system was based on one he had originated, it was possible that the lights would operate long after the tunnel was flooded.

'Hold it a minute!' Pauncho said.

They stopped. Seemingly from faraway came voices. But if they could be heard there, they would not be too far distant.

'They've probably seen our blood by now and are trailing us,' Caliban said. 'If only we could ambush some of them. They have guns and they may have first-aid kits; and they must have blacklight projectors and just possibly underwater breathing plugs.'

'Wouldn't Iwaldi know that and take care of that possibility?' Barney said.

'Yes. But we know the way, and we know what kind of traps Iwaldi has sprung,' Doc said. He did not mention the probability that Iwaldi had closed off all exits.

They went on, splashing. The water around their feet was tinged with red. Doc suddenly stopped at a corner where the tunnel ran into another. He bent over, peering, and said, 'There's Cobbs' marks.'

They went down the tunnel, turned right, walked ten yards, turned left, and were confronted with a stairway the top of which was a foot under water. The marking at the corner of the wall was still visible through the water. It indicated that the way led down the steps.

'There are three levels to go before we get to the exit,' Pauncho said.

Doc help up his hand for silence. A splashing was coming from far around the corner.

'We can't make it unless we have breathing plugs,' he said. 'And there's only one source for them. Here's what we'll do.'

Barney walked back to the far end of the tunnel and looked around the corner. Within a minute, he jerked his head back, turned, and waved at them. Then he trotted toward them. By the time he reached them, the water was up to his calves.

'Ten of them,' he said. 'Automatic rifles and pistols. Blacklight projectors on their caps but they're not using their goggles. It's impossible to tell if they have breathing plugs.'

He added, 'And I smelled smoke. The napalm can't be too far behind.'

The invaders would not know about Cobb's markings, of course, so they would go on down the tunnel. They would be looking for a way out which would not force them to submerge. Doc had looked down the corridor and seen the hole in the middle of the floor. There was a shaft there which the ancient kobolds had made apparently for quick exits, as if they were human-sized mouse holes. This was the pivotal point of his attack.

He waded down the steps until the water was up to his waist and then he swam along the wall. The bulbs along the wall guided his path and enabled Barney to see him. When Doc was opposite the shaft, Barney signaled him. Doc dived, was visible in the lights until he went under the ceiling, and then popped up in the well in the middle of the tunnel. Pauncho went down the tunnel to the end and around the corner. Doc Caliban submerged and came back up in the other tunnel. He hung on to a light bulb while Barney sat on the steps with his ear placed near the juncture of wall and steps.

In a few seconds, Barney heard the loud splashing of the ten men. He waited until he judged that the lead man was just about to come opposite the stairway, and he slid off the stairs into the water and down alongside it. When he reached the bottom, he flattened himself against the side. Now all he could do was to hold his breath and hope that the leader would take time out for a glance into this tunnel before deciding to go on. If anybody leaned out and looked down the side of the steps, he would see Barney in the light of the closest bulb.

Doc had submerged also and swam the few feet necessary to get to the bottom of the well. Here he placed one hand on the ceiling next to the lip of the shaft and waited. He hoped the bleeding would slow down enough so the men would not notice that the waters were reddened. And he hoped the enemy would not loiter in that corridor. Normally, he could hold his breath for fifteen minutes if he hyperventilated for thirty minutes (the official world's record was 13 minutes, 42.5 seconds). But he had no time to hyperventilate and he was too weakened to hold his breath for much more than two minutes.

Fortunately the lighting was such that the men above cast their shadows over the well as they passed on its right. He counted ten and swam up with all his strength as the last shadow passed. He came out of the shaft without making any noise and pulled himself with one fluid motion onto the floor. The water was then a foot and a half high and the splashing made by the men drowned out any noise he made. He stood up and quickly approached the rear man whose eyes were straight ahead. He hit him in the back of the neck and caught the rifle as it fell. By then Barney was coming down the hall behind him, and he threw the rifle to him and then waded up and knocked out the next man.

He did not fire at once. He waited until the lead man got to the corner and he saw Pauncho's long thick arm reach out and grab the rifle and pluck it out of the man's hands. The stock of the rifle, reversed, caught the man under the chin, and he went down.

Doc called, 'Freeze!'

Pauncho stuck the barrel of the rifle around the corner and said, 'Don't move!'

The shock held the others in its grip long enough for them to see that they could only die if they tried to resist. They dropped their rifles into the water and put their hands, slowly, behind their necks.

Pauncho stepped out from the corner and said, 'You there!' indicating the man now at the head of the line. 'Drop your belt! Slowly! Then get the nose plugs of this guy!' He tilted his head to indicate the man he had knocked out. This one lay face down on the floor, covered entirely by the water. He had drowned, but he would have drowned in any event, since Pauncho was taking his breathers away from him. Three men had to be sacrificed. The survivors could consider themselves lucky that they had had the right positions in the line.

While Barney kept the rifle on the men, Doc felt through the pockets of the two men he had knocked out, who had also drowned. He came up with the plugs and handed two to Barney. The enemy were dropping their belts, which held knives and pistols and bullets, into the water. At Pauncho's command, they completely undressed.

One of the men carried a medical kit. Doc opened this and popped hemenerogen tablets into his mouth. Barney swallowed some, and one man carried some to Pauncho and then returned to his place in line. There were also ointments and some pseudoprotein dressings which Doc and Pauncho applied while Barney held his rifle on the prisoners. Both immediately felt better though far from being in one hundred percent good health.

While they were doing this, the water had risen three inches.

Doc Caliban explained to the prisoners what they would have to do if they wanted to survive. They did not like the idea, but a gush of smoke and a steady rise in the air temperature convinced them that they had no other choice.

Caliban removed the ammunition from the rifles and gave one to each man. They went back to the entrance-way and down the steps, shivering at the coldness of the water. The only clothing they wore were the black-light projectors and the goggles around their necks in case they came to dark tunnels. Their captors wore only belts with sheathed knives, and they carried rifles.

The three stayed behind the seven men, who moved through the water, swimming with one hand while they held the rifles against their bellies and at right angles to the longitudinal axis of their bodies. This made for slow swimming, but it also made for safe swimming, as they found out. On the last level down, a section of the wall slid out, displacing much water as the first four men went by. Three of the rifles caught as they were supposed to do; the fourth was dropped as the man swam away in a panic. The movement of the block had been impeded by the water and the displacement of the water had warned the defenders.

There was no other incident. They reached the chamber where they had entered. By then, they were all so numb that they could hardly feel anything with their hands. Their strength was spurting out swiftly.

Doc Caliban had told his colleagues what to expect while they were getting ready to ambush the enemy. He gestured at them to make ready, and they swam to him and clung to the pipe protruding from the wall. He hoped that the massive wall of stone would slide back; the pressure of the water was immense against it. It was true that Iwaldi and his party had probably gone through this way. But they would have done so when the pressure was much less.

118

He turned the valve. The screaking of the stone against stone was shrill in the water. It hurt their ears. But the wall was moving slowly to the right, and then they felt the current as the water began to spurt out of the opening. The current became stronger as the opening widened. Doc clung to the valve until, seeing that the exit was now broad enough, he tapped the others on the shoulders. He let loose and was swept toward the opening, scraped against the edge of the still moving wall, and was shot out into the mountainside. Pauncho and Barney were close behind him.

The others had become momentarily jammed in the opening when it was only two feet wide. Then, as the wall withdrew, one went out and the others had followed. Since they had not come in this way, they did not know what to expect. They went out across the ledge and were carried over the edge and down the mountainside. This was not so steep that they were in a free fall, but the slope was rough with rocks where it was not muddy.

Caliban and his friends straightened themselves out, letting the current shoot them across the stone ledge and on down the incline. They became their own toboggans, though not without loss of more skin on their backs. The pseudoprotein that Doc had spread over his back was torn loose again, and the agony of his back would have been worse if he had not been so anesthetized by the icy water.

They managed to stop themselves by grabbing hold of bushes about forty feet down the slope. Though the water struck them hard, they held on, half-drowned and almost completely frozen. Then, frighteningly, they began to slide on down even though they kept their grips on the branches. The earth had become loosened under the pressure of the water and was now moving.

Below them came yells as their seven predecessors saw the large mass sludging above them. These men had managed to stand up, even though the water was up to their knees and threatening to knock them down and roll them for another bruising, banging slide. Now, seeing what looked like the beginning of an avalanche, they tried to run away. Their feet slid out, and they were carried away by the water and the loose mud under them.

They did not, however, go far. About forty feet further, a ledge stopped them, and they managed to grab bushes. A moment later, they screamed as the cliff of mud and rocks and bushes bearing Caliban and his aides flowed around them and then began to cover them up.

Suddenly, the flow of water became a trickle. The wall of stone had shut, and the water was penned up in the mountain again.

The seven, half-buried, struggled to pull themselves free. Caliban and his colleagues, shivering with the cold and with repugnance, took out their knives and did what had to be done. They could not afford to let the Nine know that they were here and that they had gotten free.

Just before dawn three men, covered with dried mud and nothing else, walked into the side door. Nobody saw them, which was fortunate, because the police would have been called. The three found themselves locked out, but the biggest rammed the heel of his bare foot against the door, and it flew inward with a crash. They entered, showered, shaved, ordered food sent up, dressed, and the apish-looking man went down to pay the bill. The clerk was surprised that his ugly guest no longer wore a moustache, and he noted several other lost characteristics. But he said nothing except the customary pleasantries.

The three drove off with Barney, in the back seat, operating the shortwave set.

'Trish says that Lady Grandrith has disappeared,'

Barney said. 'She tried to phone her, didn't get an answer, and went over to see for herself if anything was wrong. She saw two suspicious-looking characters hanging around and went in the back way. A guy tried to knife her on the second floor; she broke his arm and stuck his own knife in his ribs; but he got away. Clio wasn't in her room. She hadn't packed; so if she took off it was in a hurry. Trish'll keep trying to get into contact with her.'

Doc Caliban took the microphone and said, 'Trish! We'll let you know, in the usual way, when we've arrived. But you send a message to Grandrith. Tell him to come to Salisbury by way of Bournemouth. Make the arrangements; we'll have somebody meet him if he can make it. Tell him the Nine will be at Stonehenge. If he can get there, he should do so by all means. The end of the world may come if Iwaldi isn't stopped.'

Trish had a husky voice that sent delicious chills up a man's spine. 'O.K., Doc. I gave my love to Barney. Tell that big ape Pauncho I love him – like a sister. Please hurry. It's so lonely, especially since Clio disappeared. We didn't see each other, but we did have phone conversations now and then.'

'We'll be there soon. So long,' Doc said, and handed the microphone back to Barney.

'That's the first time I ever heard Trish complain,' Barney said. 'The tension is really getting her down. But then she's been through so much for so long. Ever since that nut that thought he was Tarzan kidnapped her. Things have been coming one after the other, like bad news was an endless snake, a Midgard serpent.'

Barney put on a fake beard and thick glasses and took over the driving while Pauncho and Caliban crouched down on the floor after covering themselves with blankets. Barney drove through Karlskopf slowly. If there were any agents of the Nine here, they would see only a hairy-faced old man who looked as if he taught philosophy at the University of Heidelberg. Moreover, the license plates on the Benz had been changed, so that if the agents knew the old number, they would see at a glance that this could not be Caliban's car.

Once out of Karlskopf, the two got up off the floor. Barney kept on driving, headed toward Kieselsfuss, a small town which had an airstrip nearby.

The following day, three men met near Charing Cross station. Each had come in on a separate airliner, twenty minutes apart. Each was disguised. They took the taxi to Marylebone Borough, went past the building where Clio Cloamby, Lady Grandrith, had a room, and stopped outside another building six blocks away. They were confident that they had not been tailed. They removed their suitcases and went into the building. After the taxi had left, they came out, walked two blocks, flagged down another taxi, and drove off to an apartment on Portobello Road. They were admitted by the doorman, who had been told to expect them, went up the elevator to the third floor, and knocked on Trish's door. She opened it and was in Doc's arms and kissing him, though complaining about the bristly salt-and-pepper moustache he was wearing.

'I don't have one,' Pauncho said. 'Here, give us a kiss.'

'Both of you?' Trish said, turning and grabbing Pauncho around the neck.

'Yeah, I'm man enough to make two,' Pauncho said.

'Two gorillas, maybe,' Barney said. 'Kiss me first, Trish. I come in second to no *Pan satyrus*. And speaking of pans, did you ever see an uglier one?'

'You two remind me so much of your fathers!' Trish said. She hugged and kissed them both and a few tears ran down her cheeks. 'It's almost like having them back again!'

Barney and Pauncho did not look too pleased, though

they knew that Trish meant nothing derogatory. Also, it was still difficult for them to realize that Patricia Wilde, though she looked a fresh twenty-five, had been born in 1911 and that their fathers had courted her.

Doc and the others began to remove their disguises. In a short time, they would put on others, and Trish would become a blue-eyed ash blonde, concealing her bronzish yellow-flecked eyes and deep metallic auburn hair, so much like her cousins's.

'Well, at least you don't have to conceal that superb build!' Pauncho said, as she put on a Kelly green miniskirt. 'And them legs! Whoo! Whoo!' He blew her a kiss. 'I'm sure glad you didn't inherit the Grandrith muscles!'

'I did,' she said. 'But their quality, not their quantity, as you well know, you big orangutang. Just don't ever get fresh with me again, unless I tell you you can.'

Barney grinned when Pauncho blushed. Pauncho had been high on something – vodka, which he loved on the rocks or rum-soaked pot, which he also loved, or maybe both – when he had lost his inhibitions about Trish and tried to make love to her. Trish had been in a bad mood that night – she and Doc had had an argument – and she had thrown Pauncho's three hundred and twenty pounds over her back and halfway across the room. Pauncho had acted as Krazy Kat does when Ignatz Mouse brains her with a brick, that is, as if violence and pain expressed deepest love. He had come back for more and gotten it, this time knocking plaster off the wall with his head as he sailed through the air for a short distance.

'Don't look so sheepish,' Trish said. 'You know I love you,' and she slapped him on the back. Pauncho leaped into the air, bellowing with pain. Barney laughed so hard he fell on the floor. Doc had taken off his shirt and undershirt, revealing the patches of pseudoprotein on his back and chest. He smiled slightly and said, 'Take it easy when you touch us, Trish.'

An hour later, the first one left the building. No one who had seen any of them enter would have recognized them, though the simian body and features of Pauncho and the giant body of Caliban were difficult to disguise. Doc, however, was a bent-over old man with the palsy, and Pauncho looked like a fat middle-aged man with definitely feminine characteristics. Barney wore a waxed handlebar moustache and very long sideburns. His eyes bulged out as if he had goiter disease. Trish was a blonde with a big nose and big ears.

None of their disguises were designed to make them merge into the woodwork. They did not care if they were noticed as long as they were not recognized. They left at intervals of ten minutes apart and took taxis to Charing Cross station. They went into the restrooms and when they emerged they had shed their former disguises. Now Doc was a big American mulatto tourist with a camera hung from his neck. Pauncho was a rather brutal-looking turbaned Sikh. Barney was a racetrack toff. It hurt him to dress so flashily, since he had inherited his father's delight in sartorial elegance. Trish was a bulky-bodied, wattle-chinned, dowdily dressed, middle-aged woman with messy gray hair.

As she passed Doc, she said, 'Called Clio. No answer.'

Doc Caliban took a taxi to a rental car agency and, using the forged papers and credit cards, rented an automobile under the name of Mr. Joshua King. He drove away, picked up the others one by one at different places and then drove into a large warehouse. A man wheeled several large boxes on a cart out of an office. Doc gave him some money after the boxes were loaded into the trunk of the big Cadillac.

Mr. Sargent was a tall, thin, heavily moustached, middle-aged man. He had once been one of the best safecrackers in the world, operating in the States and

England. Doc had caught him one night when he was trying to open a safe in Doc's laboratory in the Empire State Building. Doc had taken him to the Lake George sanatorium after finding out who had hired him. He had performed the usual operation, implanting a micro-circuit in his brain and then putting him through a series of hypnotic treatments. The man was unable thereafter to crack safes, even under legitimate circumstances. He got a job as a salesman for burglar alarm systems and seemed well on the way to being a completely honest citizen. But, as had happened more than once before, the ex-criminal backslid. Not into his former profession. That was forever barred to him. Sargent became a dope addict and a pusher. To raise money for his habit, he became a lowly stickup man.

Doc Caliban heard about him and again sent him to his sanatorium. He cured him of his dope habit and gave him more hypnotic treatments. Sargent went to England to work as manager of a warehouse which Caliban owned in London. (Caliban owned businesses all over the world.) He was one of Doc's most trusted agents. He had done much for Caliban when Caliban was in the Nine but the Nine did not know of his existence (as far as Doc knew).

Sargent was also the last man on whom Doc had ever operated to change his criminal ways. It was just too discouraging to implant a repulsion against one form of criminality only to have the man take up another. Or, sometimes, to go insane from, apparently, a sub-conscious conflict.

Sargent pulled an envelope from his coat pocket and handed it to Caliban. 'Gilligan not only saw them getting off an airliner, he took their photos,' he said.

Doc opened the envelope. Pauncho, looking over his broad shoulder, said, 'Cobbs! And Barbara!'

Trish looked over Doc's shoulder, too. 'No wonder

you said she was so beautiful! Makes me jealous just to look at her!'

'She looks a lot like you,' Pauncho said. 'That's why I flipped over her.'

'I heard him say he'd leave anybody, even you, for her,' Barney said.

'You should've been a lawyer like your father,' Pauncho snarled. 'The truth is not in you.'

Doc turned the photo over. On the back was the address of a Carlton House Terrace mansion.

'They left yesterday, late last night,' Sargent said. 'Crothers didn't know where. He asked around but the servants were mum.'

'Salisbury,' Caliban said.

A minute later, the four drove out with Caliban at the wheel. The trip was mainly occupied with telling Trish what had happened at Gramzdorf and with Doc going over their plans for Stonehenge. Pauncho kept coming back to Barbara Villiers as if he could not believe that she could be guilty of collaboration with Iwaldi.

'That Cobbs cat, yeah, he's pretty oily. I could believe it of him. But that Barbara, she's just too beautiful to be anything other than an angel. Besides, Doc, you haven't got any real proof! Maybe Iwaldi is forcing them to help him. They know what he's capable of; they don't want to be tortured.'

'They could go to the police,' Trish said.

'A man with Iwaldi's connections and organization could get them, police protection or not,' Barney said.

'I had Sargent check them out at the university,' Caliban said. 'A Villiers and a Cobbs are on leave from the archeology department. Their photos resemble those of the Cobbs and Villiers we know. But they're not the same. And the university said they're supposed to be digging in Austria, not Germany.'

'What do you make of that?' Pauncho said. He did not ask Caliban if he was sure. Caliban never made a statement unless he was sure or he had defined it as speculation.

An hour later, they pulled into a farm off the highway and drove the Cadillac into the barn. Leaving by the back door, they went down a tree-covered path to a small hangar on the edge of a meadow. The two men here assured Caliban that the plane was ready.

On the way, they disguised themselves again. Doc was an English businessman with brown hair and eyes, a crooked nose, and a walrus moustache. Trish became a housewife with a more conservative mini-skirt. Barney and Pauncho became informally dressed Americans.

Forty miles from the southern coast, the gray day suddenly became gray night. The plane flew into a dense fog, and from then on it was on instruments. They circled a while above the airport at Salisbury and then made a perfect landing.

'How long has this fog been here, Doc?' Trish said.

'Since two days ago. It's extraordinary for it to go so far inland for so long. The papers have been full of stories of letters from cranks who insist that a coven of witches near Amesbury are responsible for it. Or so the radio says. I wouldn't be surprised if Old Anana had something to do with it. Not with the coven. With the fog. She's the most ancient and most powerful of witches.'

They were tramping down the sidewalk to report in at the office before driving away. Trish could not see his face, so she did not know if he was kidding or not. Her cousin was not the least bit superstitious, but he admitted that some superstitions might turn out not to be such.

'Whatever is responsible for the fog,' Doc said, 'it'll suit the purpose of the Nine fine. They can hold the funeral of XauXaz without being observed. Of course, the Nine can bring enough pressure so they could get

Stonehenge to themselves even during the winter solstice tomorrow. But this way nobody will be spying on them with binoculars. The good thing about it is, we'll have a better chance to get close to them.'

'And Iwaldi'll have a better chance to sneak in a bomb,' Pauncho said.

'Everything has its checks and balances,' Barney said. 'Except maybe you, Pauncho. Aren't you overdrawn at the bank?'

'My patience is overdrawn!'

While at the airport, Doc showed an official a photo of Cobbs and Villiers and asked if they had landed there that day. The official said no, not while he was on duty. Doc was satisfied that they had probably motored down, unless the official had been bribed to deny that they had flown in, or unless the two had been disguised.

Caliban did not plan to send his people around to hotels in Salisbury and Amesbury to find out if any of the Nine were staying there. It would arouse suspicion, since it could be assumed that the servants of the Nine would be looking for too-nosy strangers. Also, it was doubtful that any of the Nine would trust themselves to a hotel. With their immense wealth, they probably owned houses all over England. These would be left unoccupied most of the time, waiting for whenever the owners needed them.

They got two hotel rooms under their aliases, Mr. and Mrs. Clark and John Booth and William Dunlap. A half hour later, a man phoned in a message for Mr. Clark. It was from a Mr. T. Lord (the T. was for Tree) and said he and his party would be arriving at Bournemouth at the stipulated time. The landing would be made at the agreed-upon spot.

Caliban called the two men in. 'We'll go up to Stonehenge late tonight after we get some sleep,' he said. 'You'll go with us, Pauncho, but you'll leave as soon as you know how to get back to us. Then you'll go to

Bournemouth. Crothers will handle the first meeting with Grandrith; you'll pick him up and bring him to us. Barney, Trish, and I and six of my men will be waiting for you to join us.'

When they awoke – having put themselves to sleep with the hypnotic techniques taught them by Caliban – they were refreshed. They ate and dressed and then left the hotel. Their equipment had remained in a rented Rolls Royce. Two more cars, filled with men and equipment, joined them. They drove away swiftly in the fog with Doc at the wheel of the first car, watching the big radar screen he had affixed to the instrument panel. They drove on A360 out of Salisbury and in fifteen minutes had slowed down for a right turn onto A303(T). They could see the signposts quite clearly when they were close because they were wearing the blacklight projectors and the goggles. Doc drove onto the side of the road near a fence a few yards past the junction and stopped. The goggles enabled them to see the ancient burial mounds, the long barrows beyond the fence.

Doc advanced cautiously, a mass detector held out before him. Pauncho held a small box with several other instruments before him, and others carried shovels and pickaxes and weapons. They went over the fence on a folding stile brought from the car and walked about twenty yards past the barrow. Here two men started digging.

Others made several trips back to the cars, each time bringing parts of a device switch that, put together by Doc, made a metal box two feet high, four feet broad, and six feet long. Two short antennae stuck out of the top of the box. The device went into a hole and was covered with dirt with the antenna tips barely sticking up.

'No doubt the Nine have already buried theirs or will soon,' Doc said. 'And if Iwaldi shows, he'll bury his somewhere around here. Which one of us activates his first is anybody's guess. But you can bet it'll be some hours before the ceremony starts.'

He stuck a device in his pocket. When the time came for it to be used, it would activate the buried equipment, which was an atomic-powered generator of an extremely powerful inductive field. In its field of influence, a cone-shaped beam with a range of a mile and a half, metal objects turned hot. Copper wires and aluminium wires would eventually melt. Gasoline was ignited and explosives were detonated because of their metal containers. Radar and heat-detectors would be unusable in its field because the circuits would melt and then the cases, if they were thin.

Doc had already ascertained that no one in the party had any metal fillings in his teeth or metal plates in his skull.

Tomorrow, when the ceremony began, the only weapons would be the baseball bats, plastic knives, crossbows, and the gas grenades that Doc had brought along. They were wearing plastic helmets and chain mail under their clothes. The crossbows were of wood and plastic and gut, a small type with a pistol-like butt held in one hand. They fired wooden bolts with a sharp plastic tips.

If the fog held, the battle would be conducted by almost blind soldiers.

Doc looked at his watch and then removed it. A man was putting everything metal in a bag which would be taken away in a car.

Pauncho shook Barney's and Doc's hands and kissed Trish before he left. He hated to go, but he did not complain. If Doc wanted him to carry out his mission, so be it.

'We won't be staying here,' Doc said, 'since the Nine will undoubtedly send men through here ahead of them. We'll be hiding out across the road north of Stonehenge. But I'll be back by the long barrow by the time you return with Grandrith's party, unless something prevents me. In which case you and Grandrith just come on up to the ruins. That'll be where it's at.'

Pauncho drove off. The other cars were driven away to a point half a mile away along A303(T) to the west. Doc figured that they would be outside the range of all three of the inductors he expected to be operating by morning. The men would bicycle back on the plastic collapsible vehicles they had brought along in the trunks of the cars. The others had been unloaded.

They waited. Presently, they heard footsteps and issued soft challenges, ready to fire if they proved to be the enemy. But the proper codeword – Pongo – was returned, and the men joined them. Then they went across the field, blindly, the wet grayness allowing them to see only a few inches. They carried their weapons in their hands and packs on their backs. These contained pup tents, which could be folded into the space of a large box of kitchen matches, and cans of self-heating food and water and medical kits.

After a walk of about four-fifths of a mile, they came to the fence along A344. They crossed it and the road and went over another fence into a field near the Fargo Plantation and The Cursus, that strange roadway that the builders of Stonehenge had made. There they bedded down for the night.

'The servants of the Nine will be poking around,' Doc said, 'but they'll probably confine their scouting to the triangle formed by the three main roads. Then the old ones will be coming in their plastic steam-driven cars – my invention, ironically enough, and made for just such occasions – and they'll start the ceremony, fog or no fog. They won't be able to bury XauXaz in the circle of Stonehenge. Not even the Nine could do that without causing embarrassing questions. So they'll probably bury him someplace close by.'

'Why hold the ceremony here?' Trish said. 'I thought XauXaz was at least 10,000 years old when Stonehenge was built. What's his association with it?'

'I don't know. Stonehenge was built in three phases from about 1900 B.C. to about 1600 B.C. by the Wessex People (so named by the archeologists). It may have been built as a temple to some deity. No one knows except the Nine. It does seem that, whatever else the rude enormous monoliths were, they did form a sort of calendar to predict seasons, and they could be used to predict lunar and solar eclipses. Those circles of monoliths and trilithons made a prehistoric computer.

'XauXaz may have been a living god of the Wessex People. He may have supervised the building of Stonehenge. His name would not then have been XauXaz, since this was a primitive Germanic name meaning *High*. In fact, our English word *high* is directly evolved from XauXaz. But primitive Germanic did not even exist then. It hadn't developed out of Indo-Hittite yet.'

After a system of guards were arranged, they got into their sleeping bags. At five A.M., Doc was awakened to stand his watch, the length of which was determined by the time it took sand to fill the bottom of an hourglass. He squatted on top of his sleeping bag by the fence for a while, then got up and walked slowly back and forth. The fog showed no sign of thinning out; he was in a cold and wet world without light. Though his party was only a few feet away, he could not see them. He could see nothing. He could hear the snores of a few men and, once, far off, muffled by the fog, the barking of a farm dog. This was the world after death, and he was a soul floating around in the mists of eternity, cut off from the sight and touch of other beings but tortured by being able to hear them in the distance.

When would the struggle stop? When would the killing cease? When would he be able to live as he wished; peacefully, studying, researching, inventing devices to help mankind?

Probably never. The only long-lasting peace was in death.

His sense of time was almost perfect. When he lit a match and held it by the hourglass, he saw that only a few grains remained in the upper part. The match went out, and suddenly the activator in his pants pocket began to get warm. He knew then that either the Nine or Iwaldi were in the area and had turned on an inductor. He removed the activator from his pocket with his bare hand, since it was not yet too hot to hold. He pressed its button and then threw it into the fog. It had done its work and its circuits would, in a few minutes, be melting.

He awoke everybody and told them what was happening. They bundled up their bags and ate a light breakfast from their cans. About fifteen minutes after Doc had noticed the activator's warmth, they heard shouts down the road.

They went over the fence, which was becoming hot, and ran across the road to the fence on the other side. After climbing over this, which was by then red-hot, they proceeded slowly along it. It was the only guide to the east. If it were out of sight, they could just as easily have turned around and gone westward or southward within a few steps.

Doc suddenly stopped and held up his gloved hand, though those behind him could not see it until they had bumped into him. More shouts and a few screams had come from ahead. He estimated that their sources were about a hundred yards away, but it was difficult to be accurate because of the distortions caused by the heavy fog. Underneath the cries was a strange note, a heavy grinding noise.

He moved on, and within a few yards he thought he could identify the strange noise. It was the growling of many dogs.

It would be a good thing to use dogs in this fog. They could not see, but they could smell, and this would lead them quickly to the enemy.

But the hemispherical devices could not be used because of the inductive fields. The metal in the circuits of the hemispheres and the controlling boxes and the wires inserted into the brains would get too hot. The dogs were being used without cerebral regulators.

His guess was confirmed a moment later when a dog yelped sharply. He went on, and then two more dogs cried out in agony. The crack of clubs against bone and flesh pierced the fog. And then a loud boom made them stop.

'They must be out of their minds, using grenades!' Trish said. 'They have to be throwing blindly!'

Doc Caliban did not think that they were so insane. As long as a group stayed closely together, so that its members knew that the others were in an area near him, they could throw the grenades anywhere else. They could hope that the little bombs would strike by chance among the enemy.

He pulled from the bulging pocket of his jacket one of the tennis-ball-sized plastic gas grenades. He twisted the pin in its north pole to the left and then yanked it out and heaved the grenade into the fog. Six seconds later, a roar and a faint orange flash came through the fog.

He removed another grenade and pulled the pin, but he never had a chance to throw it. Dark figures suddenly appeared ahead of him. And something struck him in the shoulder and spun him around.

He staggered backward then. His shoulder and arm felt as if they had been cut off. But he knew even in the shock that a bolt from a small crossbow had hit him. The plastic chain mail beneath its covering of shirt and jacket had kept the plastic point from piercing him. The shock of the impact from the bolt, fired at about five feet or so, had paralyzed his side for a moment.

He had dropped the grenade, and it had rolled to one side out of his sight. He staggered back away from where he thought it was, shouting to the others to run. They did not hear him because they were struggling with the people who had run into them.

The grenade had bounced and rolled further away than he had expected. It split the fog in a blaze of light and a wave that half-deafened Caliban. He saw the body of a man flying, turning as it arced toward him, its legs and arms spread out as if it were sky diving. The body struck near him, but the light was gone, and he could not see it.

A large man, striking out with a baseball bat, sprang at him. Doc jumped to one side, lost the man, jumped back in as the man was turning around to locate him or perhaps to make sure that no one was sneaking up on him. Doc still could not use his right arm, but his left drove in with the plastic dagger he had pulled from its sheath on his belt, and the sharp point went over the man's raised right arm and into his jugular vein. Doc stepped back, pulling the knife out, whirled in case anybody was behind him, crouched, and caught another man in the throat as this man flew out of the fog. The man dropped his crossbow. Doc picked it up – he suddenly remembered having dropped his when the bolt hit him – and he waited. Because he was still partly deafened, the sounds of battle came dimly from all around him: shouts, snarls, shrieks, bats hitting helmets and flesh or other bats, the twang of a released crossbow string, the grunt of a man hit with something.

Then a woman came running through the fog, and Doc, instead of shooting, threw himself in a football player's block at her legs and knocked her over. Then he was sitting on Barbara Villiers' chest and twisting her wrist with his left hand to force her to drop her dagger.

Another figure shot out of the fog. Doc knocked Barbara out with a left to the jaw and sprang up and rammed his head into that man's stomach.

The man went, '*Oof!*' and stagged back. A released crossbow gut twanged and the bolt touched his ear, burning it. The crossbow fell to the ground, and then the man was on the ground. Doc's left hand gripped the man's throat and squeezed just as the point of a plastic dagger drove through his shirt into the chain mail undershirt. The dagger fell, and the man choked and then became still. However, he was not dead. Even in the gray wetness, Doc Caliban had recognized the man was Carlos Cobbs. His hair was short and yellowish, and his nose was long and his chin too jutting. But the gait had been Cobbs'. Even though he had had only a second to see his manner of carrying himself, he had identified it.

Trish loomed out of the pearly mists. She put her mouth close to his ear, and said, 'You deaf, Doc?'

'Partly. But my hearing is coming back. I'm taping these two up. Get her before she comes to, will you?'

Carlos Cobbs, sitting on the ground and bending over, his wrists bound behind him, coughed and choked for a minute. Finally he gasped, 'So it's you, Caliban! I thought . . .!'

'Thought what?' Caliban said. He was squatting so he could see Cobbs' expressions better.

He had to keep twisting his neck to look around because the struggle around him, though much diminished, was still going on. From the shouts he could hear, as the victors identified themselves to others, his men seemed to be winning. Then Barney Banks appeared with the annoucement that the group they'd run into had either been killed or had run off into the fog. As far as he could tell, they had three men left who could fight, not counting Trish, and Caliban and himself, of course.

136

'You started to say that you thought that . . .?' Doc Caliban said to Cobbs.

'Never mind that!' Cobbs said. 'Let me go! And you get out of here! Fast! If you don't, we'll all get killed! I'm telling you this because I have to! Get out of here!'

'Why?' Caliban said. Cobbs did not seem to be acting; his voice shook with urgency and with dread.

Barbara suddenly sat up. She said, 'You fool! He's left a bomb back there that'll go off in fifteen minutes, in less now, and blow everybody for a half a mile around to kingdom come!'

'That right!' Cobbs said, 'It'll take the Nine with it! They'll not get away this time! Anana and Ing and Yeshua and Shaumbim and Jiizfan and Tilatoc, they'll all go out in a blaze of glory! And I, I will have done it! Listen, Caliban, we don't have time to talk about this here! We have to get going! Now! I've got plastic bicycles waiting on the road and we can get away on them to my steam cars only a quarter mile down the road and get out of here before the bomb goes off! Don't delay, man! I cut it close as it was, too close! But I didn't want them to get suspicious and take off! You know how Anana is! She's got a nose for anything that smells of death!'

A grenade cracked about forty yards behind him. More screams and yells.

Brightness dispelled some of the fog high up in the mists. (The flare was nonmetallic, of course.) Doc could see for at least a hundred feet. Shadowy figures struggled at the edge of his vision, and then, when he turned his head, the flare died.

'We could all take off and talk at my leisure,' Doc Caliban said. 'But friends of mine are out there fighting, and if we ran they'd die with the Nine. They might say that the sacrifice would be worth it. But I can't ask them, and if I could, I wouldn't. You tell me what kind of bomb it is and where we can find it. Now! Either I stop it from going off or we all die!'

'You stupid mortal!' Cobbs screamed. 'What do you care what happens to your friends if you can live forever? Listen, I can get you the elixir! I'll give you the formula! I know you've been cut off, and that the aging has started! And you'll die in a few years because you'll never have the elixir unless one of . . . The Nine gives it to you!'

'One of . . . us?' Caliban said. 'What's your part in this, Cobbs? It's obvious you're hand in hand with Iwaldi. You were just pretending to be prisoners of Iwaldi, for some reason I can't comprehend, unless it was to infiltrate into my organization and catch us all when you had us cold.'

'Time's running out!' Cobbs said, his voice cracking. 'Would you throw away eternity, man?'

Caliban reached out and pulled Cobbs' large nose loose. It came off with a slight tearing sound, and the rest of the pseudoskin over his face followed. When the wig came off, the Cobbs he knew looked out of the fog.

Barbara Villiers said, 'For God's sake, Caliban! We don't have time to play around! Get us out of here and then we'll give you whatever you want! The elixir! The map of the caves of the Nine and the traps set in it! Even some of the addresses of the Nine, though they won't go near there anymore, of course, unless they think we're all dead!'

'For two who are just candidates, or maybe just servants, you know a great deal,' Caliban said. 'Old Iwaldi must have taken you into his deepest confidences. By the way, where is Iwaldi? He wouldn't have let you go running off while he fought a rearguard action. Not old Iwaldi. He may be a mad goblin, but he's not that mad. Unless he thinks you double-crossed him figuring to blow him up with the rest of the Nine and then you two would take over. Did you plan on carrying out his ideas, releasing the phytoplankton bomb? Or did you plan to kill him so you could stop that but still get the elixir and his wealth?'

Cobbs bent over so he could get his face closer to Caliban's. His features were twisted with agony, and the moisture on his face seemed to be even heavier than the fog droplets could account for.

'Get us out of here, and I'll tell you where you can lay your hands on Iwaldi!'

'You'd betray him?'

'Why not? He'd betray anyone if it meant saving his life!'

Barbara Villiers' voice cracked, too. 'We can't tell you at this moment. He sent us in to do his dirty work for him. But we'll show you where you can ambush him. Just get us out of here!'

'What kind of bomb?' Caliban said.

'It's a heavy irradiated plastic box containing the explosive in liquid form! The dial and the time mechanism are all plastic or hard wood, too! I set it to go off in fifteen minutes! The mechanism pulls a pin out of a vial of plastic containing the gas that'll mix with the liquid and set it off! There won't be anybody living left within a half a mile radius and it'll kill many outside that area! The stone monuments of Stonehenge will be knocked down and maybe shattered! Old XauXaz's body and his coffin and the stones he set up as a temple for the sun god – himself – will be gone! Along with the rest of the Nine! Even old Anana, who said she was going to defeat death!'

'Who's fighting the Nine out there?' Caliban said. 'Or are they blundering around fighting among themselves? Grandrith can't be responsible for all that!'

'I left most of my men there to hold them, keep them occupied!'

'Doublecrossing your own men, too? Well, that's to be expected, *Iwaldi!*'

Trish and Barney said, 'What?'

Villiers gasped. Cobbs' jaw dropped.

'He can do what I can do,' Caliban said. 'He has enough control of his muscles to pull his spine and add or subtract inches to his height. I've done it plenty of times myself. It takes much practice and knowledge. But what I can do in my short lifetime, Iwaldi has had many lifetimes to learn.'

He pulled on Cobbs' nose and when that would not come pulled on the skin of the face and then on the dark hair.

'That won't do any good, you fool!' Barbara Villiers said. 'That is his own skin and hair! The old goblin you knew was the false one! The wrinkled skin and the redshot eyes and the long white hair and beard, those were the fakes! They were true enough once, but when he regained his youth – '

'Shut up!' Iwaldi yelled.

'We haven't got time to carry this deception out!' Villiers said. 'Besides, there's no sense in not telling him that we can have the rejuvenation elixir. He won't leave us here to die if he knows that he has to take us away to get the elixir! You should have known that, you greedy old man! It was our main card, and you've wasted too much time holding out! It may be too late because of your stupidity!'

'You can't talk to me that way, my dear Countess Cleveland!'

Caliban's eyebrows went up. He said, 'Then Barney was telling the truth, not kidding you as he thought he was, when he said you must be the Lady Castlemaine whose petticoats hanging out to dry made Pepys flip? Charles the Second's mistress, mother of his three sons? You did not die as history said, but you used makeup to look as if you were getting older and then you pretended to die and some woman died so that you could be buried, and you – '

'Yes!' Barbara Villiers snarled. 'Yes! How many

candidates have done that? Hundreds, thousands? You and Grandrith are my own descendents! My grandson had a child by a Grandrith woman; so I'm your many times great-grandmother! For the sake of us all, for the sake of eternal life for you and your friends, and for me, your ancestress, get us out of here! You will not only have eternal life but eternal youth!'

'I appropriated your notes, after you turned against us,' Iwaldi said. 'I knew you'd been working on rejuvenation and I hired the best scientists in world to develop the elixir from the information in your notes. One did develop it, and I got rid of him in an "accident." In two years' time, I became a young man again! The wrinkles and the white hair and the ropy veins disappeared! But I used makeup so that the others would not know! But ... must I talk away our lives! Let's get out of here! Plenty of time for talk later!'

The old man – now turned young man – knew that even if he was taken out of the explosion area, he was in grave danger from Caliban. But he was wily, and he had survived so many millennia by being more tricky than his contemporaries. He must have something up his sleeve besides sheer desperation.

'It's too late!' Barbara Villiers wailed. 'We can't get away in time now!'

'Then give me the combination!' Caliban said.

'Why not make him do it?' Trish said.

There was the sound of running feet nearby, a twang, a cry, and a man slid across the cold wet winter grass on his face. He stopped so close to Caliban that he could see the crossbow bolt sticking out of the back of his neck.

'We might not even be able to find the bomb!' Caliban said. 'Quickly, Iwaldi! The combination! It does have a combination to turn it off, I hope?'

'If I tell you, you'll kill me!' Iwaldi said. The voice of Cobbs had become the familiar deep growling voice of

Iwaldi. The panic and the cracking were gone.

'I promise to release you and Villiers,' Caliban said. 'After you give me the formulae, of course. But my word is not to be given lightly and will not be broken. I will let you two go free, give you twelve hours' headstart, after which I will try to kill you, Iwaldi. Villiers can go with you if she chooses, in which case I'll try to kill her, too. But if she wants to work with me, and I decide I can trust her, well, I don't like the idea of breaking the neck of my own grandmother several times removed, even if she's so distant I couldn't possibly have any of her genes.'

'Talk our lives away!' Villiers said. 'Iwaldi, tell him the combination! Now! There isn't much time left! He doesn't even know where the bomb is! He may not even be able to get to it in time!'

'Hey, Doc! Trish! Barney!' a deep grunting voice said somewhere in the fog. 'Pongo! Pongo!'

'Pongo! Pongo! You hairy ape!' Barney called out joyfully. 'This way!'

The squat and monstrous form of Pauncho van Veelar appeared. He rolled toward them and then stopped. 'What the hell's going on? Cobbs! Barbara!'

Barney capsuled what had happened, but Doc listened to Iwaldi.

'There are ten numbers on the dial,' Iwaldi said. 'You set the dial on each number from 1 to 10. Then go right to 3. Then back to 9. If you do that in time, you can make the mechanism push the pin back into the gas vial container. *But* you'll have to *push in* on the dial while you're working the combination. Push in hard! If you don't, the mechanism not only won't reinsert the pin, it'll pull the pin immediately. And you'll have to keep the pressure applied for five minutes after you have worked the combination.'

'Why all those provisions?' Caliban said.

'You never know when they can be used to your

advantage. Now, if I could have gotten away in time, you would have set off the explosion trying to stop it. But it didn't work out that way. Also – '

'Never mind. Later.' Doc stood up, then said, 'Pauncho, where's Grandrith?'

'Out there. I left him to find you. Why weren't you at the long barrow?'

'I sent Rickson to meet you.'

'He must've been killed before he got there.'

'Watch these two,' Doc Caliban said. 'I'm going after the bomb. Watch for Grandrith,'

He picked up a crossbow, fitted a bolt to the string and pulled it back to the third notch and locked it. Then he walked off into the fog while Trish said, 'Doc! I want to go with you!'

He did not answer. He did not want to be hampered. He ran back and forth, bent over, looking at the ground between glances on all sides. No grenades had burst for several minutes, but the crack of bats and yells were still filtering through the woody dampness. And then, as the dim figure of a trilithon – two upright stones with a third laid across them – solidified out of the grayness, he saw a body with a plastic shovel beside it. There were other bodies near it, but this one was the one that Iwaldi had told him to look for. It was that of the man who had dug the hole into which the bomb had been put. A bolt from out of the fog had caught him in the right eye as he straightened up, and he had fallen across the heap of dirt.

Caliban rolled him over and then began digging. The box was buried under a few inches of dirt, so it did not take him long to unearth it from its chalky cavity. While he was working, the grayness became luminous, as if the sun had appeared and was striving to burn the fog away. At the same time, a grenade boomed about thirty yards away, and he dived for the ground. He was up at once but heard cries from near the ruins. He faced toward the trilithon but kept on digging. Then he got down on his knees and pried out the box. It was about eleven inches square and was smooth except for the dial and the numbers around it on its top.

He had to bend close to distinguish the numbers, which was lucky for him. A bolt whizzed over his head. Two figures, interlocked, whirled by him and were swallowed up in the grayness. One of them cried out a minute later, and then Doc heard footsteps on the wet earth. He wanted to start working the combination, because he had no idea of how much time was left before the pin would be entirely pulled out of the detonating gas container. But he could not start turning the dial unless he knew that he would not be disturbed. If he had to release the pressure, he and everybody here were done for.

The man suddenly came out of the fog. Doc said, 'Pongo?' and the man cursed and jumped back. Doc could not afford to wait any longer; he fired at where the man had been, aiming so the bolt would hit the belly, if it hit at all.

The gut twanged; the bolt leaped out; a thud came; a man groaned. And immediately after, Doc heard the slight squishing of feet in wet earth and the rustle of weeds. He turned, and a giant was on him, striking out at him with a baseball bat.

Doc hurled the box at him. The man ducked but not quickly enough. He staggered as the impact sent him back, and then Doc was at him with his plastic knife in his left hand. His right arm had recovered enough for him to use it, but it was still far from having regained all its strength. The giant stepped up to him and swung with both hands on the bat, bringing it around so that it caught Doc against the side of his helmet even though he had almost ducked entirely under it. Doc saw phosphene streaks but kept on lunging, and his knife drove up. The man had dropped the club after it glanced off Doc's helmet and had put out his hands. The knife went through one; the giant roared. Doc jerked the knife out. The man brought his knee up and caught Doc in the chest. If it had hit him in the chin, it would have shattered even his massive bones. The man was wearing irradiated plastic knee guards.

The knee hurt Doc's chest and knocked the wind out of him. But his right arm closed around the leg, and he brought the knife up between the man's legs. It tore the man's pocket and slid off the plastic groinguard and then off the plastic chain mail around his leg. The man brought both fists down against the top of Doc's helmet, half-stunning him. The man howled, because the blow had hurt his fist hand. But Doc fell backward, not knowing exactly what was going on. The dagger did not fall from his hand; many years of fighting had built in a conditional reflex so that he would have had to be entirely unconscious or dead before his hand would have relaxed. And his wind quickly came back.

The giant charged in, roaring. Doc Caliban rolled over, not realizing consciously what he was doing, and he was out of sight of the man. But a few seconds later, the giant thrust out of the fog, and seeing Doc starting to get onto his feet, cried, 'No, you don't!' and rushed him, his huge hands clasped to bring them down on top of Caliban's helmet again.

Doc bent his legs and leaped outward as if he had been shot from a cannon in a circus. His head drove into the man's big paunch with an impact that did not help Doc regain his senses. But the breath went out of the man – who must have weighed three hundred and thirty – and he went backward. Stunned, Doc did not act as quickly as he should have, and the man, though struggling for breath, knocked the dagger from Caliban's hand with a blow of his arm against Caliban's wrist.

Their faces were close enough that Doc could

distinguish his features in the milky grayness.

'Krotonides!' Doc said.

He was one of the candidates, a bodyguard for old Ing. Doc had seen him a number of times at the caves during the annual ceremonies. He had endured the boastings of Krotonides that he was the strongest and fastest human in the world when it came to hand-to-hand combat and that Caliban's reputation was over-rated.

'Caliban!' Krotonides said. His dark, big-nosed, bushy-eyebrowed face hung in the fog. 'I always said I could take you!'

Caliban's hand with fingers stiffly extended stabbed him in the eye, and Krotonides bellowed with agony. He rolled away, but as Caliban got to his feet the giant leaped out of the fog, his hands in the classical position to deliver a karate chop.

Doc snatched off his helmet and threw it with all the force of his left arm and the body behind it. There was a thud, and Krotonides staggered, slowly rotating around and around, while dark blood gushed from his nose, which had been almost severed by the sharp edge of the helmet. Caliban moved in swiftly though not incautiously, since Krotonides was still a very dangerous man. Before he could reach him, three figures advanced through the mists, and he felt it discreet to withdraw. Besides, he had to get to the box as quickly as possible.

Suddenly, he heard steps behind him. He whirled and then a rumbling voice said, 'Pongo! Pongo!'

'Pongo! It's me, Doc,' Caliban said. 'Help me find that bomb before it's too late!'

The three men had been engulfed in the fog, but they were still in the immediate neighborhood, so Doc and Pauncho had to keep an eye out for them. Doc hoped that none of them would toss out a grenade in their general direction.

146

Pauncho suddenly cursed, and then he said, 'I fell over it, Doc! Hey, Doc! Quick! Over here!'

Caliban found him squatting by the box with his crossbow ready. Caliban got down on his knees and put his face close to the face of the dial. 'I'm starting now,' he said. 'Once I get going, I can't stop. I have to hang on to this for five minutes at least. So you'll have to handle anybody that shows up. But as soon as I get the combination worked, we'll run away from here. I can hang. on to the box. We'll worry about killing the old geezers some other time.'

He started to turn the dials, stopping them briefly on each number, starting with 1, advancing to 2 when the mechanism clicked at 1. He kept pressure on the dial, which had sunk within a recess about one-tenth of an inch deep when he had first pushed. He clicked the dial through each of the numbers, and at 10 reversed the dial quickly to 3 and then turned it back again to 9. On reaching this, he breathed deeply and then started to count. 'One thousand and one. One thousand and two. One thousand and three.'

When he got to 'One thousand and three hundred,' he would have counted out five minutes, but he would go to one thousand and four hundred just to make sure before he let the dial push back to its level with the box.

He stood up, holding one corner of the box with his giant hand and pressing in on the dial with the other.

'Run, Doc!' Pauncho said. 'Here comes a whole army!'

Caliban twisted his head. A number of dark figures were emerging from the fog. He said, 'Follow me! Don't stand and fight!' and he trotted away. He dared not run at full speed because he might stumble over a body or slip on the half-frozen mud. Behind him feet slapped as Pauncho kept on his heels. Somebody shouted and then about forty feet ahead of them, the fog opened up with an orange-bordered roar. Doc's feet slipped from under him as the blast hit, and he fell on his back. But he kept hold of the box and his pressure on the dial.

Pauncho was bellowing in his ear, 'Hey, Doc! Can you hear me? You all right? I'm half-deaf, Doc!'

'Quiet!' Doc shouted back.

He put his mouth close to Pauncho's ear. 'Get rid of all your grenades, and mine, too, fast as you can. Maybe you can get those guys before – '

The second grenade from the enemy was about three feet closer, and it was followed by a third which landed almost on the same spot. Since they were on level ground, the impact of the blasts was not softened. They were rolled over, and their heads sang and their ears were dead. But the plastic bombs depended almost entirely on concussion for effect, since the explosion reduced the plastic shell to dust. And they were not within the killing range of the blasts.

They would be if the enemy continued to lob grenades at random. They got to their feet and ran on. Pauncho stopped to toss grenades behind him, and Doc lost sight of him. Suddenly, he saw a body ahead of him. He tried to dodge to one side, slipped, and fell on his side. He came down heavily because his primary concern was keeping pressure on the dial. He called, 'Pongo!' and then rolled away, holding the box up, hoping that if it was the enemy it would fire at where he had been. He wasn't worried about the person tossing a grenade, since he'd be committing suicide if he threw one that close to himself.

'Pongo!' Trish said. She looked as if she were shouting, yet he could barely hear her.

He got up and approached her cautiously, since it was possible the situation had changed and she was being forced to lure him in. He preferred to believe that she would die before doing that, but she might be depending on him to get her out of the situation, no matter how bad it looked. She tended to think of him as a

148

superman, despite his lectures to her that he might be a superior man but he was also flesh and blood and one little .22 bullet or a slip on a piece of soap in the shower could make him just as dead as anybody else.

He peered through the fog. 'Talk loudly. I'm almost deaf. Pauncho may be coming along, so don't shoot without giving the codeword. Where's Barney?'

'He went after you,' she said, shouting in his ear. 'Well, not exactly *after* you. He said he was going to make contact with the enemy and explain the situation. He thought that if they knew about the bomb, and that you were trying to keep it from going off, they'd quit fighting. They might even take off and leave us alone.'

'Doesn't sound like it,' Caliban said. The crump of grenades going off in the distance – somewhere around the Stonehenge circle – was still continuing. But there were no blasts nearer, where Pauncho and the three men should have been.

Suddenly, there was a silence. From far off, as if behind piles of wood, a voice cried. It was saying something. And then another voice cried. And then he heard, very faintly – dimmed by distance or by his injured hearing, or both – a rushing sound.

'Tires,' his cousin said. 'It could be the Nine taking off in their steam cars.'

'Maybe Barney got to them,' Caliban said. 'He disobeyed orders, but he was doing something I should have thought of. Pauncho disobeyed, too, luckily for me.'

A form like a truncated monolith from Stonehenge stepped out of the fog. Trish shouted the codeword back at him. Pauncho walked up to them and said, 'Where's Barney?'

Trish told him. Doc had resumed his interrupted counting. He stared at Iwaldi and Villiers, who were standing up now. One of the three men, Elmus, was holding a loaded crossbow on them.

'It's ironic that I came here to kill the Nine and now I have to let them go, even Iwaldi,' he thought, managing to count at the same time.

Trish stopped talking to Pauncho. They had heard the squeal of tires as they suddenly accelerated and then the screams of men and the thump of a massive swiftly moving object striking flesh and bone. Then a grenade boomed, and immediately thereafter was another screech as of tires sliding on pavement. Then there was a crash, and a series of bangs. More screeches as a vehicle accelerated again and sped away. Another boom of a grenade. Then, silence.

Doc continued to count. Barney came like a ghost out of the ectoplasmic pearliness. 'I thought I'd lost you,' he said. 'I've been wandering around, afraid to go too fast or to yell out. Even though I think most of the enemy has gone. They didn't know whether or not to believe me, but they must've decided they couldn't take a chance. Besides, as one said, it'd be just the thing the crazy old dwarf would do. They think he's insane; no doubt of that.'

Doc Caliban did not ask him if he had seen anything of the Grandrith party. If Barney had, he would have said something about it.

Doc kept on counting. Undoubtedly, five minutes were passed, at least seven minutes had gone by, but he preferred not to take a chance. The blasts had hurt his head, so that his sense of timing might have been disturbed. But he could put it off for only so long, and he finally decided to take his hand off the dial. He could see Cobbs – no, Iwaldi – and Barbara Villiers watching him. When they saw his hand drop away, and nothing happened, they sighed. At least, they looked as if they had. He could not hear them. He still could hear only loud sounds.

Trish put a hand on his shoulder, causing him to jump. She put her mouth close to his ear and said,

'There's something still going on out there. In the ruins, I think. I heard a woman scream.'

They waited. There was no more evidence that a fight was still occurring among the stones, but they had a feeling that something important was taking place under the monoliths and the trilithons standing like the ghosts of the ghosts in the mists.

A faraway hoarse bellow, the cry of something not quite human, reached him. Silence again.

'You said we could go free,' Barbara Villiers said.

'Leave. Or stay here,' Doc Caliban said. 'Do whatever you wish. You have a twelve-hour headstart.'

'Untie us,' she said. Iwaldi merely glared.

'I said you could go free,' Caliban replied. 'I wouldn't feel easy with you in this fog and your hands free to pick up some weapons. Come on, the rest of you. We'll find the bicycles and then the steam car.'

'I'll come with you as far as the car,' Villiers said. 'Iwaldi told me he'd kill me because I betrayed him, though I don't know how he figures that.'

'You want to throw in with us?' Doc said. He was not inclined to trust her one bit, but she undoubtedly had very valuable information about Iwaldi's organization.

She hesitated, then said, 'Why not? I know a winner when I see one.'

'Thank you, Benedictine Arnold,' Trish said.

Iwaldi strode off into the fog. The others started to walk away, staying close to each other so they would not lose sight of each other. But they had not gone more than five steps when Doc stopped. Trish had put a hand on his shoulder. She said in his ear, 'There was a low cry! I think Iwaldi – '

They walked in the direction Iwaldi had taken. Suddenly, he was on the ground at their feet. His throat was still pumping blood through the broad wound.

Something came through the fog, and only Caliban would have been quick enough to see it and to react

151

with the swiftness of a leopard. He batted at the round object as if he were playing handball; his hand struck it and sent it back into the fog with terrific force. There was a roar. The blast knocked them all down, and his ears hurt even more, and his head felt as if it had been squeezed in a vise.

They got to their feet with Doc assisting Villiers, whose hands were still taped behind her. They went ahead slowly, and then they felt the breeze, and before they had gone thirty feet, the fog began to fall apart. The sun dropped through in pale golden threads and then the threads coalesced into a blazing ball.

A wisp of fog, like a snake, moved across the face of a man on the ground, seeming to disappear into his open mouth. Doc approached him cautiously, though the fellow looked dead. His clothes were half-ripped off by the explosion, and blood ran down from his nose, ears, and mouth. A bloody plastic knife lay near his outflung hand. His helmet had been blown off, revealing an extraordinary high forehead. He was bald, and his jaws thrust outward, giving the lower part of his face an apish appearance. His body was tall and skinny.

'I think I know him,' Caliban murmured. 'I've seen him at one or more of the annual ceremonies in the caves.'

The name would come, though it would not matter to the man, who was dead. He had come across Iwaldi and cut his throat, though he could not have recognized him as Iwaldi. But he did not know him, and that meant that he was an enemy. Then he had heard the others and tossed the grenade and it had come back so swiftly he must have thought for a horrified moment that he had bounced it off a nearby wall.

'Hey, Doc!' Pauncho bellowed. 'I think that's Grandrith inside the ruins! He's waving at us!'

OLD TIME HAS ENDED BUT EARTH IS STILL AT WAR .

BOOK 1:

Cloud Warrior

PATRICK TILLEY

Ten centuries ago the Old Time ended
when Earth's cities melted in the War of
a Thousand Suns. Now the lethal high
technology of the Amtrak Federation's
underground stronghold is unleashed
on Earth's other survivors – the surface-
dwelling Mutes. But the primitive
Mutes possess ancient powers far
greater than any machine . . .

FICTION   0 7221 8516 2   £1.95

A selection of bestsellers from SPHERE

FICTION

SPRING MOON	Bette Bao Lord	£2.25 ☐
THE AMTRAK WARS BOOK 1:		
CLOUD WARRIOR	Patrick Tilley	£1.95 ☐
THE SKULL BENEATH THE SKIN	P. D. James	£1.95 ☐
WINGS OF THE MORNING	David and Betty Beaty	£2.95 ☐
THE RED DOVE	Derek Lambert	£1.95 ☐

FILM & TV TIE-INS

AUF WIEDERSEHEN, PET	Fred Taylor	£1.75 ☐
WITHOUT A TRACE	Beth Gutcheon	£1.75 ☐
YELLOWBEARD Graham Chapman and David Sherlock		£2.50 ☐
STAYING ALIVE	Leonore Fleischer	£1.75 ☐
BY THE SWORD DIVIDED	Mollie Hardwick	£1.75 ☐

NON-FICTION

THE BOOK OF		
ROYAL LISTS	Craig Brown & Lesley Cunliffe	£2.50 ☐
MONEYWOMAN	Georgina O'Hara	£1.75 ☐
THE WORLD GUIDE TO MODEL TRAINS		£7.95 ☐
THE FINAL DECADE	Christopher Lee	£2.50 ☐
THE DOCTOR WHO		
TECHNICAL MANUAL	Mark Harris	£2.50 ☐

All Sphere books are available at your local bookshop or newsagent, or can be ordered direct from the publisher. Just tick the titles you want and fill in the form below.

Name _____

Address _____

_____

Write to Sphere Books, Cash Sales Department, P.O. Box 11, Falmouth, Cornwall TR10 9EN

Please enclose a cheque or postal order to the value of the cover price plus:

UK: 45p for the first book, 20p for the second book and 14p per copy for each additional book ordered to a maximum charge of £1.63.

OVERSEAS: 75p for the first book and 21p for each additional book.

BFPO & EIRE: 45p for the first book, 20p for the second book plus 14p per copy for the next 7 books, thereafter 8p per book.

Sphere Books reserve the right to show new retail prices on covers which may differ from those previously advertised in the text or elsewhere, and to increase postal rates in accordance with the PO.